OLIVER STORM
and the Great Disappearance

by Freddie Ellison

SJH PUBLISHING

Acknowledgements

A huge thank you to Richard Freed and Ben Duffy for making my dream of writing a book a reality, and to Julia Gray for helping me write this book and get my dream down on paper.

I would also like to thank Kerry Walsh for taking me on numerous journeys to the cities that appear in my book.

Finally, I wish to thank my parents, Katy and Daniel, and my brother, Ben, for their support, belief and encouragement.

Twenty five per cent of profits on the sale of this book
will be donated to the National Autistic Society – the UK's
leading charity for autistic people and their families.
The charity's goal is to help transform lives, change attitudes
and create a society that works for autistic people.

About the author

Freddie Ellison is a 16-year-old North Londoner who, at the age of three, was diagnosed with Autism Spectrum Condition (ASC). Freddie had problems with social interaction and communication, and a tendency to engage in repetitive behaviours, and from an early age he struggled in the education system. In March 2017, he was excluded from his school and he spent the following 18 months at home with no educational support, while his family fought legal proceedings to get him placed at an appropriate school. During this time he started writing, often several stories at once. He quickly moved into a routine of picking up his briefcase and walking down to the local Starbucks where he would pen his latest tale. SJH Publishing has committed to producing three books with Freddie, whose dream it is to one day write a bestseller that is turned into a movie.

First edition

Published by SJH Publishing
298 Regents Park Road, London N3 2SZ
020 8371 4000
sjhpublishing.org

ISBN: 978-1-906670-77-1

Cover illustration by Tayo Olarewaju

Printed and bound in the UK by CPI Books

CHAPTER 1

•

A Bit About Me

My name is Oliver. Oliver Storm. I'm fourteen years old and I have blond hair and jet-black glasses. My sister Amy is eight. She also has glasses but her hair is dark brown and curly. This is a story about me and Amy, and some other people too, and the very strange thing that happened to us, not long ago, which we call the Great Disappearance.

But let's go back a bit further first of all, so you can learn some more about me.

I grew up in a big house in a suburb of north London with Mum and Dad and Amy. Our house had lumpy white paint on the walls and reddish-brown tiles on the roof, and a green door with a silver number five. I went to a school called Phoenix Feather High, not too far from where we lived. It was a really big, old-fashioned school with lots of red-brick buildings. Dad was a teacher at Phoenix Feather High, so I saw quite a lot of him every day. He was the same at school and at home: strict, but nice to people when he wanted to be.

Life was ordinary. Life was fine. And then, suddenly, when I was eleven years old, Mum died.

I have lots of lovely memories of Mum. She had short brown hair like Amy's and a laugh that sounded like music. She liked the colour purple and she was always cheerful. She died quite suddenly. She had some kind of heart condition, they told me, though I never understood exactly what it was. We were all very, very sad about it. At first, I kept thinking that she'd just gone on holiday somewhere, like when she used to go away with my Aunt Megan to Cornwall for the weekend for a bit of a break. Every time I thought that, I felt better for a while, until I remembered that she wasn't coming back, and then I felt worse, as though there was a big grey rain cloud stuck in my head that I couldn't get rid of.

And then, just when I was starting to feel a little better, Dad did something very surprising. He got married again. I don't think he planned to, particularly, but sometimes things happen that we don't plan and this was one of those things. You'd think that maybe my new stepmother might have been one of those Wicked Stepmothers that you read about in books, but actually she was pretty and nice. Her name was Britney and she was about the same age as Mum. She had blonde hair and a lovely smile.

I thought that marrying Britney might make Dad happy again, but he still seemed very angry and very sad. We didn't get on very well, me and Dad. We argued a lot. I didn't know what to do about it and neither did he, and we didn't talk about it either, so it didn't improve.

And then, to make matters worse, I got expelled from Phoenix Feather High.

I seem to remember that it was a Tuesday. Dad was really pleased because he'd just got a big promotion. He was going to be the new Deputy Head of the school, which was a really important job and meant that he'd have his own office and more responsibility.

It was break-time and I was just going to visit the toilet before going outside to the play area. When I walked into the boys' toilets I didn't immediately notice anything strange, but then I realised that there was water all over the floor and it was spreading quickly. I went to look more closely. There were three toilet cubicles in a row. The middle one was smashed and the other two were blocked.

I looked around to see who could have done this. It seemed as though it must have been deliberate, but I couldn't see anyone around. I was just about to leave in order to find a teacher when I looked up and saw three teachers running towards me. One of them was Mrs Law, my English teacher. And there was the science teacher Mr Gupta. And in the middle was Dad.

'Oliver,' said Dad, 'what have you done?'

'I haven't done anything,' I said. 'I just came in to use the toilet. I found them like this.' All of which was true. But I could see that Dad didn't believe me. Sometimes he didn't believe me about stuff that had happened, even when it clearly wasn't my fault. This was obviously one of those times.

'You're coming with me, young man,' he said. He took hold of my ear between his thumb and first finger, which I hated because it was painful and annoying, and he walked me downstairs to the Headmistress's office. The Headmistress was a woman called Mrs Briggs. She had stylish grey hair and always wore woollen cardigans.

'Well, Mr Storm, what's going on here?' said Mrs Briggs, putting down the official-looking papers that she was reading as we entered her office.

'Mrs Briggs, I'm sorry to say that my son has flooded the boys' toilets,' said Dad, still holding on to my ear as though he was worried I'd run off somewhere.

'Oh dear, Oliver, is this true?' said Mrs Briggs.
I started to say that it wasn't true at all but then I realised that they weren't listening to me.

'I'm afraid that this means instant expulsion,' said Mrs Briggs sadly, and Dad was also shaking his head and saying that he agreed with Mrs Briggs and neither of them wanted to hear my explanation.

'This is a very unfortunate day,' said Dad sorrowfully. 'I've had to expel my own son.'

'Well, it's me who's going to expel him, actually,' said Mrs Briggs, 'since you're only the Deputy Head.'

'Oh yes, of course, Mrs Briggs,' said Dad.

•

From that point on, I was home-schooled with Britney, who had once been a teacher. She made lessons interesting and fun and I enjoyed learning with her. But I really missed going to school, so I kept asking Dad every week if I could go.

I asked him every week for nearly two years.

'You cause too much trouble, Oliver,' Dad said, over and over again. He was never going to forget about the flooding of the toilets at Phoenix Feather High. But I kept asking and asking, and eventually Britney began to tell him that she thought it would be a good idea if I went to school.

'Oliver hasn't been anywhere new in months,' she told him. 'It would be so nice for him to be around kids of his own age.'

They went into the living room and argued about it for hours, while I sat on the stairs, trying to listen. Then finally my dad came out with an angry grin that was more or less his favourite facial expression and said: 'Fine, Oliver. You can go to school.'

'YES!' I said.

The next day, Dad applied for me to go to Oakwood Academy. 'It's the strictest school in the country, they say,' said Dad. 'So if you mess up you will find yourself enduring the most horrible punishment imaginable.'

But I was really excited about it.

CHAPTER 2

•

Welcome to Oakwood

My first day at Oakwood Academy was a Monday in the middle of February. It would be the first time in forever that I would be going anywhere more interesting than the park or the shop at the end of the road, which were the only places that Dad would allow me to go. I woke up feeling full of excitement. What was my new school going to be like? Would I meet anyone nice?

Getting out of bed, I went to the window and looked out over the houses and church spires and playgrounds. On the top of a hill covered with trees, I could just see the grey towers of Oakwood Academy, about half an hour away by car. I put on the Oakwood school uniform, which Britney had ordered for me. White shirt, grey trousers, a red blazer and a red striped tie emblazoned with the Oakwood logo: a sun, a moon, an acorn and an oak tree, all in a circle. I looked at myself in the mirror and decided that I looked good in my new uniform. I'd been wearing nothing but the same too-small tracksuit for weeks now.

Going downstairs, I packed my rucksack with a jumper in case I got cold (this was the sort of thing that Mum would have made me do, so I did it for her), my iPhone, my lunchbox, with some crisps and a cheese sandwich inside, my pencil case and – after some thought – my lucky mascot, a key ring with a small replica of an Ankylosaurus from the film *Jurassic World* attached to it. There. That had to be everything I needed.

I said to myself: 'All right, Oliver, you can do this.'

At breakfast Dad was very quiet, only saying nice things to Amy which was normal because he always said nice things to Amy. He usually didn't say that much to me, but today I wasn't bothered about it because I was looking forward to going to my new school. I kept quiet and ate my porridge. Soon it was time for Dad to take Amy to school.

'Goodbye, then, Oliver,' he said to me with the same angry grin as always. 'Try not to mess up this time.'

'I won't mess up,' I said.

'I've got my eye on you,' he said. I didn't think that was really true because I was going so far away that he definitely wouldn't be able to see me from Phoenix Feather High, so I didn't say anything in reply. But

I was glad that for the first time in a long time Dad was not going to have his eye on me.

'Bye, Amy,' I called to my sister as she climbed into the back of my dad's car. She looked out of the window and waved as the car pulled out of the driveway. After the incident at my school Amy had been afraid of me for quite a while, but over the last few months we had become closer again. I was glad about this, because Amy reminded me of Mum. I didn't want her to be afraid of me. Still, she was very shy and didn't seem to have many friends. I worried about her quite a lot.

'Come on, Oliver,' said Britney, putting on her jacket and picking up her car keys. 'It's time to go. Want to get in the front?'

'Are you sure?' I said.

'Sure,' she said, smiling. 'This is a special day, after all.'

So I sat in the front next to Britney and off we drove to Oakwood Academy. There was a bit of traffic so it took longer than I'd expected, about thirty-five minutes. I watched the digital clock on the dashboard, hoping we weren't going to be late. On our way we passed a shopping centre and a humongous Tesco and brick houses, loads of them, and more shops. And then at last we had come through the town centre and went over another roundabout and after a few minutes more, we turned off the main road. Now there was a massive forest on one side of the road. And finally, we reached a pair of incredibly tall gates which had a sign on them saying WELCOME TO OAKWOOD ACADEMY. On either side of the gates, stretching away as far as I could see, was an electric fence and forest behind that was really thick so you couldn't see through the trees at all. The fence had barbed wire and snap thorns on top of it.

We stopped outside the gate and Britney opened her window, waved a pass that looked like some kind of ID card under the CCTV camera, and then the gates opened really slowly without making any noise at all and we drove through.

Just inside the gate was a security checkpoint with a guard sitting behind a glass window.

'Name, please?' he said.

'Mrs Storm,' said Britney. 'And my stepson Oliver.'

'Oh yes, of course. Good morning, Mrs Storm. Go ahead.'

Wow, I thought. That's a lot of security for a school. Anyone would have thought it was a prison we were going to. We drove through the forest, which seemed to go on for miles and miles, going slowly uphill. The trees looked like Christmas trees, only taller and thinner and without any kind of decoration. It was so dark that I almost forgot that it was daytime. I was beginning to feel a bit nervous. Just as I was thinking this, Britney looked at me and said, 'First day at your new school, Oliver. Are you nervous?'

'No,' I said. 'Well, maybe just a little.'

She laughed. 'Don't worry. As long as you don't get expelled again, I'm sure everything will be fine.'

'I shouldn't have been expelled,' I pointed out. 'I was just in the wrong place at the wrong time.'

She laughed again. 'Here we are,' she said.

I looked up at the enormous grey stone building. It was built like a sort of castle with battlements along the top and two huge towers at either end. I almost expected to see a moat and drawbridge as well, but there wasn't – just a big parking lot full of cars on one side, and what looked like a football pitch and running track on the other. OAKWOOD ACADEMY was written in big black-and-gold letters over the top of the doors, which were made of wood. Probably oak, I thought. That would make sense.

Britney parked the car. It was nearly impossible to find a space but eventually we did. Then we walked over to the main building and up a flight of stone steps till we got to the front door and I saw that there was another security checkpoint on the left-hand side. Out came a man wearing a blue suit and tie. He had a walkie-talkie attached to his belt and a guard's hat.

'Bags, please,' he said, in the sort of voice that sounded like he'd eaten a bag of charcoal for breakfast. So Britney held out her handbag and he searched it quickly as though he had done this sort of thing 4,000 times before, which he probably had, and then I gave him my rucksack.

'No outside food,' he said, throwing my lunchbox into the bin behind him which was full of other lunchboxes of all shapes and sizes. He took out another object from my bag. 'And what's this?' he said.

'That's my phone,' I said.

'All phones brought to this school must be given to charity,' he said, putting it into a box marked CHARITY. The box was full of phones, including iPhones like mine, and there was another box that had a humongous skateboard in it. I wondered who it belonged to and whether they would ever get it back.

'Right then, Mrs Storm. You can proceed,' he said.

'Aren't you going back to the car?' I said to my stepmum.

'It's all right,' said Britney. 'I'll take you inside. Come on.'

We went through the big wooden doors together and came into a massive entrance hall with a wood floor and posters stuck to every surface with the school rules written on them. Two big staircases led away to the left and right. It was really cold and gloomy and I couldn't see any students anywhere, which I thought was strange as I knew that Oakwood Academy was a big school with loads of pupils, even more than Phoenix Feather High.

'We're a little late,' said Britney. 'Tomorrow I'll make sure we leave a bit earlier. Let's go to your form room, Oliver.'

'I'm sure I can find it by myself,' I told her, but she just smiled and said, 'There's no need.'

She took me up the right-hand flight of stairs. They were really dark and made of some kind of polished wood with red carpet going up the middle. From the ceiling hung big chandeliers. Then we went along a really long corridor and there were loads of classrooms with different names on the doors, and finally we came to the end of the corridor and there was a door that said 11B.

'Here we are,' said Britney. 'After you.'

She held open the door for me and I walked in. I was already beginning to feel hungry and I was sorry that the man at the security checkpoint had taken away my lunchbox. The room was full of individual desks, not joined together at all, as though all the students were about to take a test. There were about twenty boys sitting at their desks. Some of them were reading and some were doing bits of homework. Nobody was talking. It was very strange. Then something even stranger happened. When they saw Britney all the kids got up and stood behind their chairs and looked at her really respectfully and said, 'Good morning, Mrs Storm.'

I turned and looked at Britney and I noticed that she had a badge on her cardigan that said 'Mrs Storm' on it that I hadn't noticed before.

'Good morning, 11B,' said my stepmum. 'I'm very pleased to be taking over as your form teacher. And I'd like to introduce you to my stepson, who is joining this class. His name is Oliver Storm.'

I was so surprised that for a moment I couldn't say anything at all. Britney smiled at me again. 'Are you okay, Oliver?'

'I didn't know you were going to be teaching at Oakwood,' I said.

'Well, I did tell you,' she said, 'several times. Including last night at dinner. I think perhaps you weren't paying attention. It was a happy coincidence that I got a job here to start on your first day, wasn't it?'

I didn't really know what to say, so I just stared at the floor. I wasn't sure how I felt about Britney teaching at my new school. Would the other kids tease me because of it? Or would they be nicer to me, knowing my stepmum was their form teacher? I just didn't know.

'Now, why don't you go and sit at that empty desk over there?' said Britney.

'Yes, Bri... I mean, Mrs Storm,' I mumbled. I couldn't quite tell, but I thought a couple of boys at the back might have sniggered a bit at this.

As I went over to the desk she'd pointed out, I couldn't help but think that she was probably right that I don't always listen to everything my dad and stepmum are saying, especially at mealtimes or when I'm busy thinking about other things. My dad never talks to me directly, anyway, unless he's telling me off about something. I sat down and examined my desk. It was very old and had plenty of graffiti all over it. Meanwhile, my step-mum was taking the register and talking to the class about the school rules.

'In case of emergency, always report directly to the Principal's office,' she read aloud from a laminated sheet. 'Well, that seems sensible. What else? If you want to use the toilet, you must pay £10 in cash at any designated Spend-a-Tenner machine. Oh dear, that does sound rather expensive.'

'Your step-mum seems far too nice to be a teacher here,' said the boy next to me.

I turned and looked at him. He had curly brown

hair and green eyes and was very tall and mischievous-looking. He also seemed very familiar but I wasn't quite sure why.

'Oliver Storm?' he said. 'Don't you remember me? It's me, Boris.'

Thinking about who he could be, I realised that he and I had gone to the same primary school, a long time ago now.

'It's nice to see you again,' I said, and this was truthful because I was pleased to see a familiar face. I was also glad that he hadn't asked me what happened to my mum because I didn't want to talk about it just then.

'Why are you here?' I asked him.

'Well, it's a long story,' he said. 'I may have punched a teacher.'

'Oh, I see,' I said.

'He told me I was stupid because I couldn't read very well. Which is true, by the way. I can't read very well and I am stupid. I must be. But anyway, I was annoyed that he said that in front of the whole class, so I punched him, and that was that.'

'I see,' I said again. I felt a bit sorry for him.

'That's nothing compared to what Jesse did, though.' Boris pointed at the boy on my other side, who had dark skin and brown eyes and a rather peaceful expression. 'This is Jesse,' he said. 'He set his entire school on fire!'

'It wasn't my fault,' said Jesse, who didn't look like he could have ever set anything on fire. 'It was an experiment that went wrong in the science lab.'

'Oh dear,' said Britney, who had come over to where we were sitting and was smiling down at us. 'You'll have to be much more careful in science from now on, Jesse. In fact, you have science first lesson. Off you all go, now, before you're late. And remember, no talking in the corridors. No running. No swearing. No chewing gum, and no laughing.'

So we all collected together our pencil cases and folders and went off in single file down the corridor. I went after Boris and before Jesse. Just as my step-mum had instructed us, nobody made a sound as we made our way back down the stairs and through the entrance hall where I'd come in and down some more corridors. After a while I lost track of where we were. I'd never been anywhere so big. Sometimes we passed lockers or other kids walking very quietly in other directions. We passed the toilets: one door with a toilet symbol that said PUPILS ONLY, with a machine a bit like a car-parking meter next to it, I supposed for the £10 you were supposed to pay, and then another door that said STAFF ONLY. I immediately began to feel anxious

27

because of what had happened at Phoenix Feather High – I kept expecting Dad to appear from behind a pillar and try to expel me again.

'Does it really cost £10 to use the toilet?' I whispered to Boris.

'You bet it does,' he whispered back. 'And if you don't have the money for the toilet then you have to sell your possessions. That's why I only have one pair of shoes now. And if you break any of the rules they beat you with a cane. And if a member of staff is nice to a student, they could get the sack.'

'Wow,' I said. 'That might be difficult for Britney. She's really nice.'

'You mean your stepmother? Well, we'll see,' said Boris. 'She may change.'

At the end of the last corridor was the science building. It was really big and more modern than the rest of the school. It looked like it was made entirely of metal, with enormous windows that reached all the way to the ceiling. The bell was clanging and the clock on the wall in the corridor was just striking nine o'clock as we walked into the laboratory.

The science teacher was standing in front of a massive whiteboard. He had a green blazer and a striped tie and looked very strict indeed. He looked like he definitely wouldn't mind beating kids with a cane. In fact, he probably enjoyed it. He had a name badge that said DR SISCO.

'Good morning, children,' he said, frowning.

'Good morning, Dr Sisco,' we chorused.

'You may sit down.'

I wasn't sure where to sit so I waited for the other kids to find their places before taking a vacant stool in between Boris and Jesse. 'I've not done much science,' I said to them, to make conversation. 'I've been doing lessons at home but we don't have a laboratory there, and…'

'Silence!' shouted Dr Sisco. 'This, children, is a momentously important day for the entire scientific community. In fact, it is a momentously important day for the WHOLE WORLD.'

'What's he talking about?' said Jesse.

'I dunno,' I muttered. It was all quite confusing. But we were soon going to find out.

CHAPTER 3

The Disappearance

The lab door opened and a classroom assistant wheeled in a big television on a trolley. We all stared at it. It was grey with a dark screen and two antennae on top. Dr Sisco went over and jabbed various buttons until the TV turned on. At first, the screen was all fuzzy and grey. Then a picture began to form. It was a big, dark room with a wooden floor. In the centre was a very tall, very thin man with blackish-grey hair standing next to a strange object that I'd never seen before in my life. It looked like a machine of some kind. It was grey like the TV but it was round and flat, like a massive coin, and it was sitting on sharp looking triangular feet. In front of it was a screen with a keypad, connected to the machine with a cable. The screen was glowing lots of different colours.

'Good morning,' said the scientist on the TV. He had a flat voice that seemed to suit him very well.

'My name is Professor Orwell Wells. Today marks the end of a very important period of scientific development. It has been hard. Sometimes, I have even thought about giving up. But I persisted, knowing that this is possibly the most Important Scientific Discovery that has ever been made. I, Orwell Wells, have invented a machine. I call it the MACE machine. You must be wondering what those letters stand for. Allow me to explain. It stands for Mathematicians Against Carbon Emissions. This machine, my friends, will reduce the amount of toxic carbon dioxide and other noxious gases in the Earth's atmosphere by as much as forty per cent! It will combat global warming more efficiently than any other single measure that could possibly be undertaken. All it will take is for me to press a button.'

The camera started zooming in on the machine. It looked as though it was made of some kind of highly polished metal. Now I could see the machine more closely. It had a panel full of little switches and levers and buttons and dials. It looked like something out of *Charlie and the Chocolate Factory*, except that I didn't think that Professor Wells was going to be making sweets with this machine. Could a machine really reduce toxic emissions into the atmosphere, as simply as that? I wondered. Some of the buttons were flickering orange and green and the machine emitted a low buzzing sound that got louder and louder as the camera zoomed in further.

Then there was a kind of commotion in Professor Wells' laboratory. A woman with curly dark hair wearing a bright green tracksuit burst in and ran over to Professor Wells.

'Sorry, Orwell,' she said. 'I can't let you do this.'

'Get away from me,' said Professor Wells. 'You're jealous of my success. You always have been.'

'Trust me, I'm not jealous of you,' said the woman, rolling up her sleeves.

'This machine will solve the world's most pressing problem. Global warming is a significant threat. I alone have the power to stop it,' said Professor Wells. He was looking straight into the camera. From where I was sitting in the Oakwood laboratory, it suddenly seemed as though he was staring right into my eyes. It made me feel very cold.

'On the count of three, now,' he said, in a firm, flat voice.

The woman dived towards the machine but he fended her off with his left arm, smiling as he did so.

'One...'

He flipped one lever up. The machine started to roar, like a dragon that's just discovered it's quite hungry.

'Two…'

Another lever went up. A row of buttons started flashing blue and yellow. Needles spun on dials and the word FULLY CHARGED lit up, dazzling me for a moment.

'Three!' cried Orwell Wells.

He reached out with one very thin, very long, pointy finger. And pressed the button.

For a moment, it seemed as though nothing was going to happen. And then something did.

The machine vanished.

The laboratory vanished.

Everything vanished. The screen was filled with one great big yellow wave – sort of smoky and watery at the same time. The wave seemed to get bigger and bigger each second, and my ears were filled with a kind of crazy buzzing sound.

I closed my eyes and opened them again. I thought I was dreaming or something because the room around me was also filled with a great big yellow wave. It was like walking into a rainbow and getting stuck in the yellow section. All around me I could hear kids screaming. I didn't know if they were screaming because they were frightened or because they were shocked. I closed my eyes once more and counted to eleven. Then I opened them again. The wave had faded, leaving only a kind of gentle yellow glow in small patches on the windows.

'Look!' said a boy with red hair. 'Dr Sisco – he's gone!'

We all got up and rushed towards the science teacher's desk, crowding around it, looking about as though Dr Sisco had maybe got stuck under his desk or something. But he was nowhere to be seen. Then I saw a white lab coat and a pair of trousers and two shiny black shoes and two crumpled white socks and a shirt and tie, all clumped together in a heap, just about where Dr Sisco had been standing.

'Guys, what's happening?' said Jesse.

Boris went over to the TV and stared at the screen. It was still yellow in places, but you could see Professor Wells' machine quite clearly, lights blinking, still emitting a low buzzing sound, but it was louder now. It sounded like a cat that was quite pleased at how many mice it had managed to eat.

I went over and joined Boris. We stared at the MACE machine. The camera wasn't moving. There was no one about.

'Is that what I think it is?' said Boris.

'Yeah,' I said. 'Those are Professor Wells' clothes. On the floor, next to the machine.'

'So let me get this straight,' said Boris. 'Orwell Wells has disappeared. Dr Sisco has disappeared. What is going on here? Where did they go?'

The boy with red hair came up. I realised I didn't even know his name. I didn't know anyone's names except for Boris and Jesse. 'Is this some kind of joke, d'you think?' he said.

'It's not April the first,' said someone else, joining us. 'I don't think this is a joke. Besides, Dr Sisco was never that funny.'

'We should check the other classrooms,' I said.

'We aren't allowed to leave the classroom during lesson time,' said the boy with the red hair, as though I was really stupid for suggesting it.

'Well,' I said, 'I don't think anyone's going to stop us, somehow. You coming, Boris? Jesse?'

I could feel everyone watching the back of my head as I walked towards the door. As I had predicted, nobody stopped me. Opening the door, I realised I could hear something unusual. There were science classrooms all along the corridor and they were all filled with the sound of kids talking. Not teachers. Not grown-ups. Kids.

Bang!

All of a sudden, my foot got caught in something lying on the floor. Tripping, I went tumbling headlong through the air and ended up with my head in a bucket of soapy water.

'Oliver, are you okay?' said Jesse, rushing over and helping me up. 'You'd better sit down and rest for a while. You might have concussion.'

'I'm fine,' I said, but I thought it was kind of him to be so concerned about me.

'Look,' said Boris, pointing at the pile of grey clothes in a heap in the corridor. 'The caretaker – he's gone too.'

'Where *is* everybody?' I said, using the caretaker's overalls to wipe soap suds out of my hair.

'Not everybody,' said Jesse. 'Just the teachers. And the caretaker. It's the grown-ups. They've gone.'

'They have to be somewhere,' said Boris. 'People don't just disappear.'

Boris, Jesse and I walked kind of slowly down the corridor back towards the main building. We kept passing classroom after classroom where the same scene was unfolding – kids standing around a pile of clothes, looking scared, looking confused, looking excited at the prospect of freedom. Some students were doing stupid things like swinging from the light fixtures and running in and out of the toilets without paying the obligatory £10 each time.

'That gives me an idea,' said Boris suddenly. Going to a Spend-a-Tenner machine, he gave it a swift kick or two, and then chortled as the machine groaned and fell over. Wrenching off the lid, he took out a massive pile of £10 notes.

'Cashback!' he grinned. 'Always good to have some money on you in case of emergencies. That's what my dad always says.'

He slowed down and looked at me and Jesse with a strange expression on his face. 'Oh my God,' he said. 'My dad. Do you... d'you think our parents have gone too?'

Jesse and I didn't say anything for a moment. I shot a glance at Jesse. He was looking really upset. I wasn't upset, though. I was sure Dad could cope with disappearing just fine. If Mum had been alive, that might have been different. But then I realised something. Amy! What if she was at Saint Hearts right now with the same kind of crazy chaos exploding all around her? Amy didn't like sudden loud noises. She needed me. Right now.

'I have to go,' I said. 'I need... I have to go and find somebody.'

And before they could say anything I was off, rushing down the corridor, hoping I'd be able to remember the way.

CHAPTER 4

•

The Principal's Car

Slipping through the crowds of newly liberated Oakwood Academy students, I retraced my steps until I got back to our form room. It was empty. Wherever all the other kids were, it wasn't here. I could hear shouts echoing from the assembly hall, and doors slamming. Going to the teacher's desk, I looked everywhere for Britney's clothes. At first, I couldn't see them. But then, there they were – her red skirt and white blouse and smart jacket, and the twisty floral scarf she always wore – in a neat pile just beside her chair. The sight of the clothes of somebody I actually knew, as opposed to a teacher like Dr Sisco, who I'd never met before today, made my stomach do a couple of strange back-flips. I knelt down by Britney's shiny navy leather shoes, which were lying awkwardly at right angles. Then, carefully, I put them side by side. Britney would like that.

I went and got my rucksack from the hook where I'd hung it up and automatically looked inside for my iPhone. But it wasn't there. Of course! They'd taken it away at the security checkpoint. Well, I'd have to get it back. I looked for my wallet but it wasn't there either. I remembered Dad had told me there was no need to have any money on me at my new school. Typical Dad, not to have known about the Spend-a-Tenner machines. Or else maybe he knew and just didn't care. But my lucky mascot was still there, and that was good. I needed all the luck available.

'Oliver!'

I looked up to see Boris and Jesse standing over me.

'Guys,' I said, 'you really don't need to look after me. I'm fine. I'm just leaving to get my sister.'

'Where is she?'

'Saint Hearts Junior School,' I replied, not that I could see how it was any of their business.

'And how are you planning to get there?' said Jesse.

'I...' Actually, I hadn't got that far with my thinking. 'I was going to get a bus.'

Boris was casually opening Britney's handbag.

He took out a tube of Werther's Originals and unwrapped one.

'See,' he said, 'that might be tricky, since there won't be anyone to drive it.'

'I'll walk, then,' I said.

'That'll take you hours,' said Jesse. 'And besides, you won't be able to get out of the school gates. Not without an exit code.'

'So what's your strategy?' I said.

'We need to get to Principal Brown's office. All the key cards and security codes are in there. At least then we'll be able to get out of the building.'

I didn't see what other options I had, and besides, I liked Jesse, and I quite liked Boris, although I didn't like the fact that he was eating my stepmother's Werther's Originals.

Minutes later, we were our way back down towards the main hall, where Principal Brown's office was. All of a sudden, Jesse slowed down and said, 'Wait, guys. Can you hear that?'

At first, I couldn't hear anything. Then I realised what he meant. There it was again. *Knock, knock, knock*. We were just passing a big room with DETENTION CENTRE written on the door. Boris opened the door and we went in. Inside, it was like a prison visiting room, with a chair and a phone and a small square window, and another chair and phone on the other side. There was a kid – younger than us – banging on the glass.

'Johnny!' said Boris. 'I was wondering where he'd got to.'

'Who's Johnny?' I said.

'My brother,' Boris replied. 'I should have realised he'd be in detention, 'cause that's where he almost always is.' He went over and picked up the phone and shook it a few times. It obviously wasn't working. Then he started miming Don't-Panic-We're-Coming gestures at Johnny through the glass. Johnny looked a lot like Boris. He seemed thoroughly annoyed at being stuck in detention and was mouthing 'Hurry up' through the window at his brother.

'We need to get the key card from Principal Brown,' said Jesse. 'Boris, you wait here with Johnny. Oliver and I will go to the Principal's office.'

Principal Brown's office was at the end of a long corridor next to the assembly hall. The door was locked.

'Oh, great. Now what do we do?' said Jesse.

'How do we know he was even inside when the yellow wave hit?' I said.

'He always spends Monday mornings in his office,' said Jesse. 'That's when he looks at everyone's behaviour charts from the week before and sees

41

how much money he's made from the toilet charges and stuff. Sometimes he calls staff members into his office and fires them if they've been too nice. That sort of thing.'

He tried the handle of the door again, rattling it so hard that it nearly came off in his hand. 'We really need to get inside,' he said. 'Without the key card, we won't be able to get out of Oakwood Academy. Or rescue Johnny.'

'OK,' I said. 'No problem.' I leaned against the door experimentally. Good – it didn't feel as though it was bolted. Then, reaching into my rucksack, I rummaged around until I found my lucky mascot – my silver Ankylosaurus. Ignoring Jesse, who was being quite annoying and asking what I was doing every few seconds, I carefully unwound the wire of the key ring until I had a fairly straight length of wire about fifteen centimetres long. Perfect. Then, slowly, I slotted the wire into the keyhole and jiggled it around – it's not easy, picking a lock, but it's not impossible either – until there was a tiny, pleasing 'click'.

'Woah!' said Jesse. 'How did you know how to do that?'

'Just beginner's luck,' I said modestly. In actual fact, I'd had quite a bit of practice. Since Dad had locked my bedroom door every night for about two years, I'd had to get quite creative about ways to go downstairs and watch TV while the rest of the house was sleeping.

The Principal's office was crammed with books – mostly on punishment and discipline and rules and things like that – and framed certificates. There was a big desk with two leather chairs on one side, probably for parents to sit in, and a high-backed armchair on the other. On the floor by the fireplace there was a now-familiar pile of clothes. Nodding at the sad-looking heap of polyester, I said: 'Principal Brown?'

Jesse nodded back. 'And that dress looks like it belonged to Miss Hope, the Head of Maths. She was new. And quite nice. He was probably firing her.'

I looked down at the green dress and brown boots on the carpet that had once belonged to Miss Hope and wondered again where all the adults had actually gone. There was a landline on the Principal's desk. I grabbed the receiver eagerly, thinking that the sooner I could call Amy and tell her I was on my way, the better. But there was only a fuzzy, static-y noise and no dial tone. Weird.

Jesse had picked up Principal Brown's trousers and was going through the pockets. 'Bingo!' he was saying. 'Key ring... key card... yeah. This is all we need.'

Back in the detention centre, Jesse pressed the key card over the scanner. The door to the holding cell where Johnny was waiting slid open. Out came Johnny. Although he was younger than us, he was tall for his age and full of energy – exactly the kind of kid who ends up in detention a lot, but then gets even more frustrated because his energy has nowhere to go. He bounded towards us, his hair flying in all directions, saying: 'What's happening? One minute I'm just sitting here in detention. The next minute the room goes as yellow as cheese. I didn't know what was going on. I've been pounding on the window for ages, waiting for somebody to come.'

I realised that, underneath all that energy, he was a little bit frightened.

'It's OK,' said Boris, patting Johnny on the shoulder. 'I'm here now.'

Johnny stared at me. 'Who's this?'

'This is Oliver,' said Jesse.

'What was the massive yellow cloud thing?'

'We don't know,' said Boris. 'There was a scientist on TV. We were all watching. He had a kind of machine... He said he was going to reduce carbon emissions in the world's atmosphere, or something. And then everything went yellow, and the adults all disappeared.'

Johnny frowned, and then laughed. 'No, they didn't. That's ridiculous.'

'Look for yourself,' I said. There was a whole row of screens on one wall, showing different parts of the school – the detention rooms must have doubled as a kind of surveillance centre. 'See? No adults anywhere. And see those heaps of clothes dotted about the place? That's all that's left.'

'Oh,' said Johnny. 'So… now what do we do?'

'I don't care what you guys do,' I said, 'but I'm going to Saint Hearts to get my sister Amy. She's only eight and she'll be really scared right now.'

'We're coming with you,' said Jesse. 'We ought to stick together. But first, let's pick up some supplies.'

•

When we got to the cafeteria it was clear that everyone had had the same idea as us, because the chiller cabinets were almost empty. We picked up a handful of sad-looking apples and oranges and bottles of water and put them in our rucksacks, just in case. A few people were sitting around, eating sandwiches and talking in low, excited voices. I didn't see any big groups anywhere. It wasn't like in *Lord of the Flies* when all the kids got together and formed a big unit after their plane crashed on the island. No one seemed to want to be in charge. Still, I felt curious about what the other kids were thinking about or planning to do next.

When I saw the boy with the red hair, who was sitting with a couple of other boys building a pyramid of Coke cans, I said: 'Are you staying here, or what?'

He shrugged. 'Yeah, I guess so.'

'Why?'

'I've already been expelled twice from other schools,' he said. 'If the adults come back soon – and I'm sure they will – they'll be furious if we've broken any rules.' He looked nervously at the Coke cans. 'I shouldn't even be doing this, really.'

'Bunch of wimps,' said Boris, leading the way as we left the cafeteria.

Next, we went to the security office where – it seemed like a whole lifetime ago now – the security guard had taken away my iPhone and lunchbox earlier that morning. It was a bit like a museum in the security office. A giant archive full of confiscated goods. Sweets, gadgets, games... I couldn't believe how much stuff there was. Boris was cheerfully helping himself to fistfuls of everything, while Jesse reminded him in a firm voice that he shouldn't be taking things that belonged to other people.

'I guess we should be quick,' said Boris, reluctantly putting down an enormous box of Quality Street.

'If the adults do come back, I want to be out of here before that happens.'

'Agreed,' said Jesse. 'Let's find our phones and get out. How do you think they sort them?'

'Here,' I said, pulling a black box down from a shelf. 'It's marked 11B. That's our form.'

Inside the box was every kind of phone you could imagine. I recognised mine straight away because it had a thin crack across the top-left of the screen from where I'd dropped it a couple of days before. I turned it on, typed in my passcode, and waited impatiently for the home screen to appear. But when it did, I saw that there were no signal bars. I dialled Amy's number anyway – hers is one of a few numbers that I know perfectly from memory, and even though she wouldn't have her phone switched on in school, at least I could have left a message. But it was no good. Just like the landline in the Principal's office and the phone in the detention centre, my iPhone wasn't working.

Next to me, I could see the same thing was happening to Boris and Jesse. Johnny, meanwhile, was looking out of the window towards the car park with a thoughtful expression on his face. (I didn't know Johnny well enough at that point to know that this was his mischief-planning expression.)

'Is your iPhone working?' said Jesse.

'Nope,' I said.

'I reckon Professor Wells' machine did something to the networks,' said Jesse. 'The yellow wave knocked out the phone lines.'

'Maybe you're right,' I said. I certainly couldn't think of another explanation. 'How long d'you think it'll take us to walk to Saint Hearts? A couple of hours?'

'Yeah, probably,' said Boris. He looked around. 'Where's Johnny?' he said.

For a split second, I saw him scanning the floor for a pile of clothes. He's scared that Johnny's disappeared too, I thought.

'The Principal's key ring's missing!' said Jesse. 'I was sure I put it down just here...'

'Calm down, both of you,' I said. Then there was a hooting noise from outside the window. We looked out and saw Johnny, grinning from ear to ear, behind the wheel of a huge pale blue car that looked really old and quite cool, from the 1950s maybe. Leaning out of the window, Johnny called out: 'Fancy a lift?'

'Oh my God,' said Jesse. 'That's Principal Brown's car. Johnny must have taken the keys.'

'All RIGHT!' yelled Boris, climbing out of the window.

Jesse hesitated. 'We aren't old enough to drive,' he said. 'If someone catches us...'

I thought about this. I agreed with Jesse, really: I didn't like the idea of doing something that was against the law. But, then again, I really wanted to get to Amy as quickly as possible.

'Come on, you guys!' called Boris from the car. 'No one's going to catch us. The adults have gone. We can do anything we want to.'

Jesse thought about this for a while. Then he smiled. 'Like naked basketball!' he said. Boris rolled his eyes and said, 'Maybe not absolutely anything.' Then Jesse and I climbed out of the window and jumped down into the car park.

'We must all wear our seat belts,' I said, approaching the car. It really was a very interesting-looking car. I didn't know much about cars but Principal Brown obviously liked them. I hoped it was road-worthy.

'All right!' said Johnny, sounding exactly the same as his older brother. 'Pedal to the metal and let's get OUT OF HERE!'

CHAPTER 5

•

A Trip to Tesco

I don't know whether Johnny actually knew how to drive or if he was just making it up as he went along, but he certainly seemed to have a lot of confidence. I wondered how he was even managing to reach the pedals. I supposed he had very long legs for an eleven-year-old.

At the car park exit, the old car sailed through the security barrier like a tank. Bits of splintered wood flew off in all directions. Johnny and Boris whooped and yelled as we zoomed down the hill towards the road, picking up speed every second. Jesse had his eyes closed. Through my window, the pine trees were blending into a thick green blur. Was Johnny going to smash through the solid wooden gates that I'd passed through with Britney earlier that morning? But it seemed even Johnny wasn't that crazy. He stopped as we neared the main gates, with a huge screech of brakes, while Boris hopped out to tap the Principal's key card against the scanner.

'Next stop, Saint Hearts Junior School,' said Boris, jumping back in.

We drove along for a while, then, as we got to a roundabout, Johnny said: 'Guys, I think we may have a problem.'

Looking at the road, I could see what he was trying to say. There were stationary cars here and there – not many, because it was no longer rush hour – but enough to make it kind of tricky to navigate our way through the streets. I hadn't thought of that. It seemed that the yellow wave really had made *all* the adults disappear. Not just the ones in buildings, but the ones out walking their dogs, or sitting in buses or behind the wheels of their cars.

'Luckily this is a quiet area,' said Johnny, as we threaded our way past empty buses and taxis and motorbikes lying sadly on their sides. 'We'd better avoid the city centre. It'll be impossible to get anywhere.'

'I reckon lots of adults were at home, watching Professor Wells on TV,' said Jesse. 'That's why the streets aren't more full of cars.'

Boris started rummaging in the glove compartment. Eventually he found an old London A-Z. Opening it, he began to map-read, slowly at first. I remembered how he'd told me he wasn't good at reading. But after a while he had worked out where we needed to go, and how we could avoid the most congested roads.

I was starting to feel anxious at the thought of not being able to reach Amy quickly. Jesse seemed to realise, because he said, quietly, 'Don't worry, Oliver. We'll be there soon.'

•

By the time we reached Saint Hearts my heart was thumping so loudly that I was sure the others were going to be able to hear it. As soon as Johnny pulled up alongside the school, I was out of the car and running towards the entrance. It was a different kind of school to Oakwood Academy. The gates were standing wide open and there was no security checkpoint.

'We'll just wait here,' called Jesse as I ran through the playground, passing the swing set on one side and the massive trampoline on the other. It was completely deserted.

Now I really was panicking. What if Amy had gone? What if all the kids at Saint Hearts had decided to leave, and had swept Amy away with them? I reached for my lucky Ankylosaurus and I felt its comforting silver spikes, just for reassurance, as I ran through the door to the main school building. I'd only visited Saint Hearts twice – once for a poetry recital and another time for their Christmas play – and I'd never seen Amy's form room. I'd just have to find it.

The school was so different to Oakwood, I kept thinking. It was a school for children with Special Educational Needs. Amy had been diagnosed with autism when she was five. There were colourful paintings by students on the walls, and friendly signs saying WELCOME in lots of different languages. Everywhere I went, I kept calling: 'Amy! AMY!'

My footsteps were as loud as my heartbeat as I ran down corridor after corridor, peering into every classroom as I went. Still no sign of Amy. Every so often I passed tell-tale clumps of adult clothing. At last I saw a couple of boys of about Amy's age running the other way.

'Hey!' I said. They didn't slow down as they passed me, but one of them looked at me curiously. 'Have you seen Amy? Amy Storm?'

'Nope,' said the boy, hurrying after his friend. I was just about to turn back and follow them to see where they were heading, when I saw something I recognised. There, hanging from a hook at the bottom of a twisting staircase, was Amy's coat. It was a plastic raincoat, purple with bright pink dots. Amy loved purple because Mum wore it so often. And next to the coat was Amy's rucksack. I opened it, just to check. Yes – inside was the picture of the four of us that Amy always carried with her. So Amy must still be inside the building, I thought. There was no way she would have left without her stuff. It wasn't like Amy to do that.

Grabbing the coat and the rucksack, I ran up the stairs, three steps at a time, still calling Amy's name. WELCOME TO YEAR 4, said a giant yellow-and-green banner at the top of the stairs. Good. I was definitely in the right place. There were two doors to Year 4 classrooms at the top of the stairs. I opened one and peered in. Nothing. I tried the other one and got the biggest surprise of my life – well, perhaps the second-biggest surprise of my life (since the yellow wave probably still counted as the biggest).

Amy was standing on the teacher's desk with a very strange expression on her face that I'd never seen before. She was smiling a weird, faraway smile that made her look completely unlike herself but also, at the same time, a little bit like Mum. She had both arms raised above her head like a ballet dancer, or perhaps an orchestra conductor. And all around her there were things floating in the air. Pencils. Books. A Sellotape dispenser. Highlighters of all different colours. For a moment, I was so amazed that I just stood in the doorway, watching. I realised that Amy was controlling the flying objects with graceful sideways motions of her hands.

'Amy!' I said.

She looked at me, startled, and at once all the objects clattered to the floor. Then in an instant she'd scrambled off the desk and was running towards me.

'What on earth were you doing?' I said to her at the exact same moment that she said, 'What on earth is going on?' And then we looked at each other and shook our heads and said: 'I don't know!' and then we started laughing. And then we stopped laughing.

'They've gone,' I said. 'All the adults. Did you watch the professor on the TV?'

'What professor?'

'Professor Orwell Wells,' I said.

'*The* Professor Wells?' said Amy excitedly.

'Wait, do you know who he is?'

'I've seen him on YouTube,' she said. 'He's a very clever particle physicist. Some people think he's a bit crazy, though. Tell me everything that happened on TV.'

'Come on,' I said, handing over her coat and rucksack. 'We've got a car outside.'

As we walked, I tried to explain about Professor

Orwell Wells and his MACE machine and his experiment that was broadcast live on television to the world. Amy is probably the smartest and most logical person I know. (As well as being the only person who could, apparently, make objects fly, but that was such a strange development that I wasn't quite able to deal with it yet). She listened while I was talking, occasionally wrinkling her nose to show that she was thinking.

'So,' she said. 'He was trying to reduce carbon emissions? That's what he said? And then all the adults were gone? In a big yellow wave?'

'Yeah, that's right,' I said. We were crossing the playground.

'That's very interesting,' said Amy. 'It suggests two possibilities, doesn't it?'

I had no idea what she meant. 'Did you see the wave?' I asked her.

'Of course. We'd just finished lining up at the end of morning break. Mr Flatly was leading us back inside when there was a kind of muffled booming noise – really hard to describe – and then everything was covered in a giant yellow cloud. And when the cloud cleared, Mr Flatly was gone. There was just his suit and tie and shoes on the ground. Nobody knew what to do. The phones weren't working. Eventually most of the kids decided just to go home. They mostly live quite close to school.'

'So why didn't you leave?' I said.

She looked up at me. 'Because I was sure you were coming to get me,' she said, in a way that made me feel very full of love. 'Also,' she added, 'I didn't want to go home if there wasn't anyone there. No Mum, and no Dad.'

'Yeah,' I agreed. 'Not that Dad ever seemed to like me much anyway. Even when he was there.'

By this time, we had nearly reached the car. 'I'll introduce you to everyone,' I said. Amy could sometimes be a bit funny around people she didn't know well. 'You'll like them, don't worry.'

'Are they all boys?' said Amy, sounding doubtful.

'Well, yeah. But they're really nice. I promise.'

As I was saying this, I was thinking that I didn't really know Boris and Jesse and Johnny all that well. I hoped they were nice. But I couldn't be sure. I was also thinking that maybe it would be good if we could meet a couple of girls to join our... group? Gang? I wasn't sure what we were, all of us, yet. I made up my mind to ask the next nice-looking girl I saw if she wouldn't mind coming along with us.

Wherever we were going.

'That's an amazing-looking car,' said Amy, cheering

up at the sight of the pale blue car gleaming in the cold February sunlight. But when we got to the car, we saw that there was nobody inside. 'That's weird,' I said.

'They've left you a note,' said Amy, pulling a scrap of paper from the windscreen. It said: GONE SHOPPING. 'It'll be the giant Tesco down the road,' said Amy wisely. 'That's where Dad takes me to do the weekly shop, after school every Thursday.' She looked sad, and I wondered if she was missing Dad. It was difficult for me to miss him in the same way, but I understood that Amy probably felt differently about him.

It turned out that it wasn't just Boris and Jesse and Johnny who had gone to Tesco. As Amy and I walked through the glass doors (not the revolving ones, which didn't seem to be working, probably because a few grown-up shoppers had disappeared and left all their bags stuck inside it), we saw what seemed like hundreds of kids milling around in the aisles. Some were riding up and down in trolleys. Others were slithering about in pools of melted ice cream and having popcorn fights. It was mayhem. Amy doesn't like loud and chaotic places so she immediately hung back and then stayed very close to me as we wandered about, looking for the others. 'Where are your friends, Oliver?' she muttered.

I looked for Boris and Jesse and Johnny but couldn't see them. 'I don't think they'll be in the fruit and vegetables aisle,' I said as we walked.

'They're probably getting non-perishable goods,' said Amy. Sometimes she uses words that I don't understand because she reads a lot, especially books about science and nature and technology. 'Things like crisps and biscuits that don't need refrigerating,' she explained.

But Boris and Jonny and Jesse weren't in that aisle either. Eventually we discovered them in the DVD section. Boris was holding an open box of Krispy Kremes and occasionally taking enormous bites out of a doughnut. 'Hey, you made it!' he said to me and Amy. 'This must be your sister. I'm Boris. That's my brother Johnny over there.'

He pointed to where Johnny was sitting cross-legged by a display case full of DVDs. '*Robocop*!' he said, adding a DVD to a pile on the floor. 'Sweet! I've always wanted to watch it. And the *Jurassic Park* box set and *Miss Peregrine's Home for Peculiar Children*.'

'And I'm Jesse,' said Jesse. 'Would you like a Krispy Kreme, Amy?'

But Amy doesn't like Krispy Kremes so she shook her head and looked a bit shy.

'Hey, Johnny!' yelled Boris suddenly, making Amy jump. 'Want to play a game?'

'Sure,' said Johnny, getting up.

'Take a trolley, grab what you can, and first one to the checkout wins,' said Boris.

'All right!' yelled Johnny.

Jesse smiled and said that he'd better be the umpire. He made sure that Boris and Johnny were lined up exactly side by side in the aisle. 'On your marks, get set... GO!' he shouted.

Boris and Johnny went clattering away, the trolley wheels squeaking loudly as they zigzagged down the aisle. I watched as Johnny swept more DVDs into his trolley: *Beauty and the Beast*, *Kong: Skull Island*, *Power Rangers*, *Logan*, the *Back to the Future* trilogy, *Paul Blart: Mall Cop 2*, *Alice in Wonderland*... Meanwhile Boris was collecting video games. *Grand Theft Auto*, *Mortal Kombat*, *Mario & Kirby*, *Donkey Kong*... Without even meaning to, I started following them to see where they would go next. Now they'd reached the sweets. Every kind of chocolate and candy bar imaginable went into the trolleys. Next it was the frozen aisle for ice cream and frozen pizzas.

Amy was sort of laughing and frowning at the same time. 'It's too much,' she was saying, 'but it's quite funny, I guess.'

Suddenly Boris wheeled his trolley around, shouting, 'I forgot the pick 'n' mix!' Johnny was laughing so much that he could barely steer his trolley, which was groaning under the weight of all the stuff he'd taken from the shelves. I watched as Boris ran over to the pick 'n' mix, hands outstretched greedily. Then, to everyone's surprise, a girl stepped out of nowhere. She must have been standing quietly in the sweet aisle the whole time, saying nothing. She had a purple jacket and a pink shirt and pink boots, the same colour as flamingo feathers. Her hair was bright orange. She looked about my age.

'STOP!' she said. 'What do you think you're doing?'

It was funny: she wasn't older than us, and she was hardly dressed like a teacher or any kind of person in authority. She wasn't even talking very loudly, yet there was something in her voice that made Boris come screeching to a halt. He stood there, one arm still pointed hopefully in the direction of the sweets, looking at the orange-haired girl with a guilty expression. 'We're... shopping,' he said.

'No, you're not. You're looting,' she said. 'You're taking property that doesn't belong to you. That's stealing.'

'Oh, yeah?' said Johnny, making his way over with his piled-up trolley. 'Do you own Tesco or what?'

'No, I don't,' said the girl. 'But my mum raised me to believe that stealing is wrong.'

'Well, she's not here now, is she?' said Johnny. I noticed he wasn't sounding quite so brave and defiant. 'There's no adults anywhere,' he went on. 'So we can do what we like. And you can't stop us.'

Then Boris amazed me by saying: 'No, she's right. We do have to pay for what we take. It's not the same as the school cafeteria. Come on, bro.'

And then – quite quickly, considering how much stuff they had in their trolleys – Boris and Johnny (who was still protesting a bit that it wasn't fair) took out everything apart from a pile of frozen pizzas and two or three DVDs. Then Boris wheeled the trolley over to the checkout and pulled a pile of £10 notes from his pocket and put them carefully next to the till.

'There,' he said.

'Thank you,' said the girl. 'Every little helps.'

Boris looked confused by that, but I didn't because I recognised it as an old advertising slogan used by Tesco in the 1990s. I laughed and the girl looked at me and Amy, who was still hiding behind me.

She said, 'Don't be frightened,' and Amy came out from behind me and said quietly to the girl, 'I'm glad you made them pay for what they took.'

'Hey,' said Boris to the girl, 'you should come with us. You can't just stick around in Tesco all day. I'm Boris, by the way.' He reached forward, as though to shake hands with the girl. She looked down at his hands, which were plastered in melted chocolate and bits of doughnut. He wiped them on his trousers while the girl gave him a cool nod. 'I'm Emma,' she said.

One by one, we introduced ourselves. I was pleased that we'd found a girl to join our group. Now Amy wasn't the only one. Maybe she'd come out of her shell a little more.

'We should find a place to stay,' said Jesse. 'It's going to get dark soon, and it'll get colder, too.'

'He's right,' said Boris. 'I don't think we can go to anyone's house. There won't be enough room for all of us.'

'And besides, it'll be strange without our parents,' whispered Amy, who I think was still really missing Dad.

'Don't worry,' said Emma. 'I know a place.'

•

CHAPTER 6

The Holiday Inn

And just like that, Emma joined our group. With her bright orange hair and her bright pink boots, she was easy to follow as she strode out of Tesco – Boris and Johnny scurrying to keep up – and into the car park. Now we were six, and that was good, because not only did we now have a second girl in our gang, but also six was Amy's favourite number.

'Hurry up,' Emma said bossily to Jesse, who stopped briefly to tie his laces. 'We all need to stay together. People are beginning to behave like savages. It isn't safe out in the open for long.'

'Where are we going?' said Boris to Emma.

'The Holiday Inn,' she said. 'We'll be safe there. It's very secure.'

'Awesome!' I said. 'I love Holiday Inns.'

It was true: they are my favourite brand of hotel. I like the fact that no matter which Holiday Inn you go to, you can always be sure that lots of things will be the same, like the logo and the type of pillows and the furniture in the rooms and so on. Whenever we went on holidays as a family before Mum died, I was always pleased if we stayed in a Holiday Inn. Amy squeezed my hand tightly as we walked back to the car and I could tell she was thinking the same thing.

Jesse didn't sound convinced, though. 'A hotel?' he said. 'How are we going to get into the rooms?' He dangled Principal Brown's key card in front of his nose. 'This isn't going to be much help, is it?'

'Don't worry,' said Emma. 'Just trust me. Where's your car?'

'It's parked over the road at Saint Hearts,' Boris said. 'It's our dad's.' This was a lie, of course. Clearly Boris didn't want Emma to tell him off for stealing the Principal's car.

'You'll like it,' he went on, proudly. 'It's a proper vintage Sunbeam. Very rare model from 1957. In spectacular condition.'

This did not sound like a lie. Boris clearly knew quite a bit about cars.

'I'm the designated driver, by the way,' Johnny said. It seemed that they were both pretty keen to impress Emma. 'I've got a better sense of direction than Boris.'

'You do not. I'm just letting you drive to keep you quiet,' said Boris.

'Hey!' said Johnny, cannoning into Boris and sending him staggering across the pavement.

'Stop it!' said Amy and Jesse at the same time. By now we'd reached the Saint Hearts car park.

'Look,' said Emma, pointing. 'Isn't that a 1957 Sunbeam driving off down the road? What a strange coincidence!'

Boris and Johnny stopped fighting immediately. Johnny said, 'Oh my God! That's... our car!'

It was true. It was hard to be sure, but the two boys grinning like lunatics in the front of the car looked a lot like the kids I'd seen running around Saint Hearts while I was looking for Amy. The car swung three times around a mini-roundabout, as though the thieves couldn't decide where they were going, and then zoomed off into the distance and out of sight.

Johnny felt frantically in his pockets, then looked up with a miserable expression. 'I must've left the key in the ignition.' He shook his fist at the car as it disappeared, just the way people do when they're really angry on TV.

'You total idiot,' said Boris.

'I loved that car,' said Johnny. I could see that he was trying not to cry.

'Now how are we going to get to the Holiday Inn?' said Jesse.

'Walk,' said Emma. 'It's only about twenty minutes.'

The others all made groaning noises. I thought for a minute and then said: 'Guys, I have an idea. Boris, can I borrow twenty quid?'

'Sure,' said Boris, taking his stack of £10 notes and peeling off a couple.

'Wait here. I'll be right back,' I said, and sprinted back across the road towards Tesco.

Minutes later we were all equipped with our own personal shiny skateboards. 'They were on special offer,' I said to Emma. 'I've always had a good eye for a bargain.'

'Very good,' said Emma. 'I'm impressed.'

'I'm not,' said Johnny. 'It just won't be the same as Princi... as Dad's car.'

'Any wheels are better than no wheels,' said Jesse. And off we went, travelling in pairs: Boris and Emma, the Johnny and Jesse, and me and Amy at the back. Amy and I used to go skateboarding together a lot when we were younger. She had a blue skateboard with Little Mermaid stickers on it and I had a green one with Jurassic Park stickers on it. As we rolled along together, concentrating on keeping our balance, I thought about how strange it was that we were spending a Monday afternoon in this way. The streets were weirdly quiet, and I realised it was because all those noises that are caused by adults doing things, like driving cars and buses and so on, were absent. You could really hear the birds in the trees, and the occasional high-pitched screams of kids running free. We passed a VUE cinema and a Hollywood Bowl and a Pizza Hut, a McDonald's, a Wagamama and an Ask, which is my favourite Italian restaurant. The sight of all these food places was making me very hungry. I hoped Johnny and Boris had enough frozen pizzas for all of us. It's always annoying when you're sharing pizzas and there isn't quite enough to go around.

It was just beginning to get dark as we crossed over a narrow canal bridge and then came to a big, brightly lit forecourt with a fountain in the middle. There was the Holiday Inn, looking wide and welcoming with all its lovely identical windows and potted plants on either side of the tall glass doors.

'Welcome,' said Emma.

'Ha!' said Boris. 'You sound like you live here or something.'

'I do,' said Emma, pulling a key card from her pocket. 'My mum is the manager. Or rather, she was the manager until she disappeared. I guess I'm in charge of the place now.'

I looked at Emma with new-found awe and respect. Here was a girl who was in charge of her very own hotel. A Holiday Inn, no less. I couldn't imagine anything cooler.

'Just relax while I get us checked in,' said Emma.

'Oh, don't bother with all that,' said Boris, going over to a huge fish tank full of clownfish near the lifts.

'Safety regulations,' said Emma. 'We need to know who's in the building at all times.'

'She really likes rules, doesn't she?' I said to Amy as Emma went over to the computer at the check-in desk and started registering us on the system.

'Rules keep you safe,' said Amy. She was also looking at Emma with awe and respect. Johnny slithered across the polished floor and then started jumping on the leather sofas. Then he fell backwards, rather dramatically, and complained that he was so hungry that he was going to faint. Emma told him where the hotel kitchens were. 'Just make sure you wash your hands,' she said.

'I'll go with him,' said Jesse, and off they went with the stack of frozen pizzas, saying they'd be back soon.

Emma had her own living quarters in a separate part of the hotel but she booked the rest of us into the nicest suites that the Holiday Inn had to offer. Amy asked if she and I could have room 111 (because she knew how much I like the number 11) and Emma said that was no problem, because it was free.

'They're all free, actually,' she said. 'There were no children staying last night. I can see on the system that twenty-six rooms were occupied this morning, but all the guests were adults. So I guess they're all gone now.'

It was indeed totally and utterly silent in the Holiday Inn. There wasn't even any music playing in the lobby. I helped Amy to fill in the forms with our names and addresses, and then Emma swiped a fresh key card through a machine and handed it over with a dazzling smile.

'I hope you enjoy your stay with us,' she said.

'Oh, we will,' I said.

'This is the life,' I said, as Amy and I sat side by side next to the ginormous swimming pool on the top floor of the Holiday Inn, each with a perfectly cooked pizza on a paper plate next to us. Boris was swimming noisily up and down, while Jesse and Johnny were practising dives at the end of the pool. Emma had lent everyone swimsuits and swimming trunks from the hotel gift shop.

Emma was looking at me with an amused expression. 'Aren't you curious about where the adults have gone?'

'Not really,' I said.

'Good riddance!' shouted Boris, mid-length. 'Who cares where they are?'

'I do,' said Amy.

'I do, too,' said Emma.

'Well, I expect they'll be back sooner or later,' I said, eating the last of my pizza. It was ham and mushroom, which is not my favourite variety of pizza but still perfectly acceptable. 'In the meantime, I have absolutely no problems staying at this delightful hotel with all you delightful people for company.'

'What about when we run out of food?' said Emma.

'We can get more from Tesco,' I said.

'And what about when Tesco runs out of food?'

'I... oh.'

Emma had a point. I hadn't thought about the fact that Tesco would no longer be getting deliveries from suppliers as long as there were no adults.

'We can always grow food,' I said.

Emma laughed and said she liked my optimism. But Amy wasn't laughing. As I've said already, my sister is very smart and very thoughtful and she often thinks about the wider picture in a way that other people sometimes can't. As Boris and Johnny and Jesse splashed up and down, shrieking with delight, I looked at Amy and wondered what she was thinking about.

'Hey, Amy,' I said. 'You OK?'

She got up suddenly. 'Emma, can I use the computer at reception?' she asked.

'Of course,' said Emma, handing her a fluffy white robe and matching slippers.

•

Amy is the sort of person who needs to see things for herself. So I should have guessed that she'd want to watch Professor Wells operating the MACE machine and see exactly how the yellow wave happened. Pretty soon, she and Emma and I were sitting in front of the Apple laptop at the hotel reception desk, looking for footage of Professor Wells' experiment. At first, it seemed like we weren't going to be able to find it. It wasn't on BBC iPlayer even though the actual programme had been broadcast earlier that day on BBC1.

'I guess it wasn't uploaded by the channel,' muttered Amy, typing very quickly as she always does. 'The adults disappeared, after all. So there was no one to update anything. But there's a chance... yes, there's a small chance... Here we go.'

I peered at the screen. She was on YouTube now. Yes: there was the TV studio from that morning, with Professor Wells standing in front of his machine. But the angles weren't exactly the same, and the footage was shaky, not steady.

'Someone was filming this as they watched it on TV,' said Amy, watching carefully. 'On their phone, probably. Uploading to YouTube simultaneously.'

Emma was looking at the screen with interest. 'I didn't see this either,' she said. 'I was doing homework in the lobby. What a weird-looking guy.'

'Professor Wells is a genius in many respects,' said Amy.

'Shh,' I said. 'I want to hear what he's saying again.'

We all listened as Professor Wells said, 'This machine, my friends, will reduce the amount of toxic carbon dioxide and other noxious gases in the Earth's atmosphere by as much as forty per cent! It will combat global warming more efficiently than any other single measure that could possibly be undertaken.'

'This,' said Amy, 'is clearly a lie.'

'What do you mean?' said Emma. 'You mean, he was trying to make the adults disappear?'

Amy frowned. 'He's a very good scientist. I think he did what he set out to do. So, yes. He wanted to make the adults disappear.'

'But why?' I said.

'I'm not sure,' said Amy.

'Oh my God,' said Emma. 'I can't believe he was

allowed to do it.'

'He wasn't,' I said. 'He tricked the TV channel. He tricked everyone. Look. The woman in the green tracksuit is trying to stop him.'

We watched in silence as the woman burst in to try and prevent the professor from pressing the button. I found myself desperately wanting her to succeed even though I knew she wouldn't. Next to me, Amy was holding her breath.

'One... two... three!' cried the mad professor. There was a dull thud, like someone falling off a bunk bed. And the screen went cloudy yellow, and then, abruptly, the video ended. For a while, nobody said anything. It had been truly bizarre to watch Professor Wells and his MACE machine for a second time. Amy played it again, skipping forwards and backwards as though looking for something. Then she paused the video.

'I know that woman,' she said, frowning. 'I've seen her before somewhere.'

'What woman?'

'The lady who comes in to stop Professor Wells,' said Amy. 'She's also a scientist, I think. She's written books on particle physics. Her name's Charlotte... no, Catherine... I can't remember.'

Emma yawned. 'Guys,' she said, 'it's getting late. I'm going to show you to your rooms.'

'Just a minute,' said Amy. She was looking carefully at the screen. 'This YouTube channel is registered to someone called TEO2004.' She scrolled through some of the other videos. 'Make-up tutorials, book reviews. Look, she's a teenage girl.'

Emma and I glanced at the screen. Sure enough, the person calling herself TEO2004 was a Chinese girl who looked a little younger than us, with long dark hair and a determined expression.

'I'm going to send her a message,' said Amy.

'Why?' I asked.

'Because she's posted this video for a reason,' said Amy. 'Maybe she knows something we don't.'

•

Amy's and my suite was on the first floor, just across the corridor from the others'. I'd never stayed in a suite before. It was massive, far bigger than a typical Holiday Inn family room. There was a lounge area with two sofas, a TV and a mini bar, and then a huge bedroom with twin beds and some very nice pictures of boats in a harbour on the walls. There was a shelf of books that could have been chosen for me and Amy: *Alice in Wonderland* by Lewis Carroll and *Peter Pan* by J. M. Barrie and all seven of the Harry Potter books and

The Hobbit and *The Lord of the Rings* by J. R. R. Tolkien and every Roald Dahl book like *The BFG* and *Matilda*. There was even a bowl of sweets on the table – a definite improvement on a boring old basket of fruit. I helped myself to some cola bottles, picked up *The BFG* and lay back, enjoying the fluffiness of my towelling robe.

Amy was standing by the window, looking out into the wintry night.

'What are you doing?' I said.

'Saying goodnight to Dad,' she said, 'wherever he is.'

'Ah,' I said.

We brushed our teeth with the hotel's complimentary toothbrush kits and wondered whether we'd be able to borrow some clothes from Emma the following day.

'Emma's nice,' said Amy.

'They all are, really,' I said. 'Goodnight, Amy.'

'Night, Ols.'

In the dark, looking at the shadows on the ceiling, I realised she'd called me by the name she used to use for me, when we were much younger. So that was one good thing about all of this – that Amy and I were getting to know each other again. I didn't miss Dad, but I was beginning to wonder how he was. Was he OK? Dad liked his creature comforts, like a squishy sofa and a cold bottle of beer in the evening. Yes: I didn't miss him, but I hoped that he was all right. Then I fell into a deep and perfectly dreamless sleep.

CHAPTER 7

•

The 328 Bus

I woke up to find various items whirling around the room: the TV control, a box of tissues, our rucksacks and a Holiday Inn hairdryer. I looked over at Amy's bed. She was fast asleep with an eye-mask on. Amazing! She was controlling flying objects and she wasn't even awake. I'd always thought my sister was special, but this was something else.

Cautiously, I went over and touched her shoulder. 'Hey, Amy,' I whispered.

At once, she sat bolt upright and the objects dropped to the carpet. 'Wow,' she said, blinking a little in the morning light. 'Was... was that me?'

'Yes.'

'How very interesting. I don't remember being able to do this before.'

'You definitely couldn't,' I said.

'I was having such an odd dream,' said Amy,

reaching for her glasses and putting them on. 'It was a cold, dark room – a bit like the one with the MACE machine in it, but this time there was no machine. Professor Wells was there, and some other people. They were very, very angry. Somebody was crying and saying: "We've simply got to find them!" and Professor Wells was shrugging and saying he was sorry but he didn't think there was anything that anyone could do. What do you think that means, Oliver?'

'I... I have no idea,' I said.

'What's for breakfast?' said Amy, after a while. I could tell that she didn't want to think about her dream any longer.

'Sweets,' I said, indicating the bowl on the coffee table.

'Yum!' said Amy.

We dug in. There were lollipops, gummy bears, Haribo mini cola bottles, chocolate eggs and short sugary liquorice laces. Every delicious thing imaginable.

'I wonder if anyone else is up,' I said.

Someone knocked on the door just at that moment. I went to open it. Emma was standing in the doorway, looking as though she'd had a pretty good night's sleep. She was holding a basket full of laundry with the reception desk laptop balanced on top of it.

'Hey, guys,' she said. 'Room service. Here's your clothes from yesterday. I've washed and pressed them.'

'Great!' I'd been wondering about clean clothes. I don't like wearing the same socks two days running. 'Thanks, Emma.'

'Just leave a nice review on TripAdvisor when this is all over,' said Emma, with a wink and a grin. Amy assured her that we would. Amy went to have a shower and get dressed, leaving me and Emma to chat for a while, which was nice. I asked Emma which school she went to and she told me that she didn't go to school at all; she was home-schooled with her cousin at the Holiday Inn. Then I went to have a shower, while Amy and Emma ate more sweets.

'Oh look, Amy,' Emma was saying when I came back. 'You've got an email.'

We all sat around the laptop, eating sweets, and read the message:

My name is Teodora Yang. My mother is Dr Caitlin Yang. She's a government scientist. She's the one in my video. Mum used to work with Professor Wells at her lab in Bristol. She knew he was planning something terrible with his MACE machine. She tried to stop him but she couldn't.

'Dr Caitlin Yang!' said Amy. 'That's right. She works in the field of quantum physics, I think. I've read some of her articles. Sometimes she's on TV. So this girl is her daughter. I'm going to message her back and ask her where she is.'

'What's that noise?' said Emma, looking out of the window. Joyful beeping was echoing from the forecourt of the hotel. Joining Emma at the window, I looked down and saw a big red 328 bus circling the courtyard. Then, suddenly, it stopped with a massive screech, and Johnny leaned out of the window. Clearly the kid had a real thing about driving.

'Guys!' he yelled. 'Check out my new ride.'

•

'So,' said Johnny from the driving seat, about fifteen minutes later, once we'd packed up our stuff and checked out of the hotel. 'Where are we going?'

'Luton Airport,' said Amy at once.

We all looked at her. 'Why?' I asked. 'What's at Luton Airport?'

She tapped the laptop. 'Teodora Yang, that's who. She's trapped there. We need to rescue her.'

'And, um… I'm sure she's a lovely person, but why, exactly, do we need to rescue her?' said Jesse.

Amy said: 'We need to rescue Teodora because her mother was trying to stop Professor Wells.'

'Who?' said Johnny.

'The man who made the adults disappear,' I reminded him.

'Teodora can take us to her mother's lab. Hopefully, if we try hard enough, we'll find out how to get to Professor Wells' MACE machine.'

'And do what with it?' said Boris.

'Bring the adults back, of course.'

'Why would we want to do that?' said Johnny. 'Adults don't let you drive before you're seventeen.'

We were nearly at the motorway now. There was thick grass on either side of the road, and a forest beyond. I peered out of the window and suddenly saw three or four kids dressed as wolves, sitting on a bench. They had wolf masks and even T-shirts with a wolf's head on them. Next to them was something made out of branches. It looked like some kind of cage... I shuddered. The wolf-kids looked menacing and scary and I was very glad that we were travelling past them quickly. One of them saw me looking, and snarled.

'Were those kids dressed as wolves?' said Emma.

'Yeah,' I said. I turned to the others, because I could tell that Boris and Johnny (and maybe Jesse, I wasn't sure) weren't convinced. 'That's why we need to get the adults back,' I said. 'Kids are turning savage, really fast, and who knows what will happen if we don't restore order to the world?'

'OK, OK,' said Jesse. 'I'm in.'

'Me too, of course,' said Emma. She looked at Boris. I knew he wouldn't want to disappoint Emma. 'Me too,' he said, a little reluctantly.

'Johnny?' I said.

'Yeah, yeah. At least let me get some good driving in first. Next stop Luton airport,' said Johnny, flicking on his indicator and turning right onto the slip road that led to the M1. 'Oh no, you guys!' he moaned.

In front of us was a gigantic lorry lying on its side. It was blocking the whole width of the entrance to the motorway. Johnny jammed the brakes on.

'We're going to crash!' Emma screamed.

'No, we're not,' said Amy. She was incredibly calm. She half-closed her eyes and scrunched her hands into fists, then she raised them above her head, slowly but decisively. She was concentrating really hard, I could tell. Was she trying to move the lorry? But it was massive!

Then the view from the window shifted; the grass tilted onto a diagonal and we began to float upwards. I could hear the bus engine groaning. Emma seized my hand and didn't let it go.

'What the...?' said Boris, hanging on to the seat in

front. 'This… this is so cool! Has Amy always been able to do this, Oliver?'

'No,' I said. 'Just since yesterday morning.'

The 328 sailed upwards in a huge arc, easily clearing the lorry that was lying in its path. For another twenty metres or so it glided forward, then it began to come down again. With a bump and a squeal, the bus landed on the motorway. It bounced a couple of times and zigzagged crazily from side to side… I hoped none of the tyres had burst. But after a few seconds the bus seemed to stabilise.

Amy was quite pale next to me, with little droplets of sweat just under her hairline.

'That was amazing,' I said.

She opened her eyes and replied: 'It really was. I do surprise myself sometimes.'

CHAPTER 8

•

Luton Airport

'Luton's one mile away,' announced Johnny, as the bus cruised down the M1.

'Oh!' said Emma, looking concerned.

'What's up?' I asked her.

'What do you think happened to the aeroplanes when the yellow wave hit?' she said. 'What if they all just... fell out of the sky?'

There was a silence in the bus while we all considered this.

'It's possible,' said Amy, glumly.

Sure enough, as we got closer to the airport, we saw the wreckage of fallen planes – just a couple of aircraft here and there. Emma winced and looked away.

'Wejusthavetohopethereweren'tanykidsonboard,' I mumbled.

'Here we are,' said Johnny, swinging onto a slip road and following signs for the short-stay car park.

'I'm staying behind this time,' he said. 'No one's going to steal my wheels again.' I could see that he had already grown quite fond of the 328 bus.

•

I'd been to Luton airport before and remembered it as a crazy, noisy place full of light and movement: people in a hurry, shoppers stocking up on small-size toiletries and aeroplane snacks, massive queues to go through security. As we walked into the airport now, our footsteps echoing on the floor, it was like some kind of ghost town. No one at the check-in desks. Just puddles of clothes and abandoned suitcases. No announcements on the Tannoy. Even Boris, usually the boldest of all of us, was moving slowly and cautiously, as though he wasn't really sure what might happen.

'Where are all the kids?' asked Jesse.

'Maybe there were no kids here yesterday morning,' said Emma. 'It was a Monday, remember? They'd have been in school.'

'Not all of them,' said Jesse. 'Not the ones from abroad coming on holiday. Maybe they left. Or maybe they're hiding.'

I looked around. There were trails of crisp packets

and drinks cans leading out of WH Smith, showing that kids had definitely been through. Some suitcases had been opened and rummaged through. It was weird – even though there was no one around, I still had the strangest feeling that we were being watched.

'Finally, Wi-Fi!' said Amy, sitting down at a cafe table outside Costa and tapping out another message to Teodora. 'I hope she's online.'

We all helped ourselves to muffins and sandwiches from Costa (Emma carefully checking the use-by dates on the packets and Boris leaving some money by the till, because Emma had told him to) and waited for Teodora's message.

Pretty soon it arrived: 'I'm at Gate 28. Go through security and follow the signs. But be careful.'

Amy typed: 'Stay where you are. We're coming.'

Going through security was very strange. I was so used to queuing for what felt like years, creeping along at a snail's pace to go through the scanners. Now we all just walked through. I was worried that Amy's laptop would trigger an alarm as she walked through with it under her arm, but it didn't. Clearly the machinery wasn't working any longer. Or maybe the MACE machine had disabled it. When we came out into the departures area there was more evidence that kids had been there: I could see smashed glass and scattered boxes in Dixons, and clothes hanging off their hangers in Next. Something that looked like paint was splattered in giant blotches on the floor. But there was nobody about.

'We need to get to the gates,' said Amy. 'There should be a sign...'

We looked around. There were some signs: toilets, baby change, quiet zone... I could see Gates 1 to 6 and 7 to 12, but no 28 anywhere. So weird. Then I realised that some of the signs had been graffitied over in paint. It looked like a word or a slogan. SAPPHIRE FOREVER, it seemed to say, in splashy blue writing.

'Guys,' I said. 'I think the Gate 28 sign has been vandalised.'

'Okay,' said Amy. 'There are four possible routes. We'll just have to try all of them. Shall we split up into groups?'

'NO!' we all said.

'Listen,' said Emma, holding up one hand. 'Music. Coming from the executive lounge.'

'Oh, cool,' said Jesse. 'I love executive lounges.'

'We need to get to the gates,' said Amy.

'Let's just have a look,' I said. 'There might be someone in there who can help us.'

Boris strode ahead and pushed open the door to the executive lounge. At once, the music became louder – I recognised it, but I couldn't remember for the moment what it was. The place was a mess. All the food had gone from the buffet area; there were spilled drinks and discarded trays all over the place. There were bottles of beer scattered about and ashtrays filled with cigarette ends in the smoking area.

'Someone's been having a massive party,' said Boris.

I could see that the big leather chairs had been slept in because there were pillows and blankets still on the seats. But the lounge was deserted... apart from two boys. They must have been about twelve or thirteen, I thought. One had blond hair and a red leather coat. The other had brown hair and was wearing a black suit with a pink shirt. They were sitting side by side at a massive rectangular table that must have been used for big groups or meetings or something. They were watching a movie on a big laptop and eating a ginormous bowl of popcorn. They looked very scruffy, as though they hadn't had a shower for days and had been sleeping in their clothes.

They didn't look up as we approached. In the end, I waved a hand and said, 'Uh, hello? Guys?'

Not taking his eyes from the screen, the brown-haired boy said, 'I'm sorry, but there's no room.'

A bit baffled, we all looked at each other.

'What do you mean?' said Emma in her bossiest voice, looking at the empty chairs around the table. 'There's plenty of room.'

The boys started chuckling hysterically, still chomping on popcorn. 'Didn't you hear?' spluttered the blond one. 'There's no room.'

Now they were laughing so much they couldn't speak. Suddenly I understood why they were behaving so oddly. They were watching the remake of *Alice in Wonderland*, a film that I really liked and had seen many times. Clearly, it had made them decide to act like the Mad Hatter and the March Hare.

'Gentlemen,' I said, 'we are trying to find Gate 28. Do you know which way we need to go?'

'Why is a raven like a writing-desk?' said the blond one, stuffing another handful of popcorn into his mouth. 'That is surely a better question.'

Amy stamped her foot. 'We don't have time for this, Oliver!'

'Wait,' I said. I'd had an idea. 'Okay, guys,' I said to the two boys. 'You obviously like riddles, right?'

They nodded. 'Mad about them!' said the brown-haired one. 'I'm Luke,' he added. 'This is Freddie.'

'How about this. I ask you a riddle. If you get it wrong, you have to tell us how to find Gate 28. Do we have a deal?'

Freddie surged forward and shook my hand enthusiastically. 'Oh, yes, my good man!'

Suddenly serious, Luke whispered to him: 'Wait. I don't think we should agree. Remember what we're meant to be doing... I don't think he'd like it.'

I wondered who they were talking about. They argued quietly for a while. The movie had finished and the credits were rolling up the laptop screen. Finally, Luke and Freddie turned to me and said, 'Ask us your riddle.'

Feeling in my pocket for my lucky Ankylosaurus, I closed my eyes and thought hard for four seconds. I loved riddles. It had to be guessable, but hard... At last, I had it. Slowly, I said:

'Sometimes I fly, but have no wings.

There's lots of me, but I have no weight.

I cost the same for thieves or kings.

Without me, you'll be very late.'

Freddie and Luke looked decidedly puzzled. The gentle sound of popcorn being crunched and swallowed filled the silence.

'A dragon?' said Luke.

'Don't be absurd,' said Freddie crossly. 'They have wings.'

'Oh yeah.'

'Air!' said Freddie. 'It has no weight... it can fly...'

Now it was Luke's turn to be critical. 'Air can't fly. You fly through it. Idiot!'

'One more guess,' I said.

'This is so difficult,' they grumbled in unison.

'Oh, I know!' said Luke.

'No, you don't.'

'Yes, I do. It's TIME!'

Delighted, they high-fived each other. I felt terrible. My plan had backfired. I hadn't thought they were going to be able to get it. Now what were we going to do?

'That was most entertaining,' said Luke. 'We'd like to thank you for your kindness in asking us this riddle. Gate 28 is the very last gate. You'll find it's a nine-minute walk. Out of the lounge, turn left, then left again into the corridor and all the way to the end. Mind the paint. It's still wet in places.'

As we left, they were still giggling and eating and arguing over which movie to watch next.

'That was... super-weird,' said Boris, leading the way as we marched along the dirty carpet towards the gates.

'How did you know how to deal with them, Oliver?' said Emma.

I shrugged. 'They've obviously been watching movies since the yellow wave hit. I could see that they actually thought they were characters in *Alice in Wonderland*. I reckoned the only thing to do was to ask them a kind of *Alice in Wonderland*-style riddle... and it worked. I wasn't sure. Especially when they actually got it right.'

'You know,' said Jesse thoughtfully, 'I think they were guarding the departures lounge. In a way. They were on the lookout.'

'But what were they looking out for?' said Emma.

'I dunno,' said Jesse. 'Intruders, maybe. Like us.'

We were jogging now. I couldn't explain it, but I had the strangest feeling that someone was watching us. The same graffiti was scrawled across posters and benches. SAPPHIRE FOREVER. What did it mean? Was it to do with the person Luke and Freddie seemed to be working for?

'Wait, guys,' said Amy, slowing down. 'I don't think this is...'

Pfffft!

We stopped dead in our tracks. 'What was that?' asked Boris.

Pfffft!

'Ouch!' Suddenly Jesse was hopping up and down, his hands clamped over his ankle. 'Something just bit me!'

Emma knelt down and looked at his ankle. 'That's

not a bite. It's a wound. You've been shot by something. A slingshot, I think.'

Pfffft! With a little scream, Emma collapsed into Jesse. 'They got me in the shoulder. Everyone, run!'

But Amy was screaming too. 'Not this way! The other way! It's a trap! Look at the gate numbers!'

She was right: just above our heads was a sign for Gate 14. We'd been given the wrong information by Freddie and Luke. Either because they were nuts, or because they'd been told to misdirect anyone who came by. They'd sent us to a place where someone was lying in wait, ready to fire... Boris grabbed Emma's hand and I supported Jesse as we hurtled helter-skelter in the other direction. Now the gate numbers began to increase. 23, 25... Someone was still shooting at us. I could hear the sneaky, whistling sound of slingshots being fired to our left and right as we ran. Eventually the shooting stopped and we began to slow down. Emma was crying again.

'Don't be upset,' said Amy.

'I'm not upset,' said Emma. 'I'm furious. What has happened to everyone's manners?'

'We're here,' said Jesse. 'This is it. Gate 28.'

Staying close together, flinching in case someone started shooting again, we gazed around the gate. Empty seats. Adult clothes. Abandoned backpacks and briefcases. Sweet wrappers and crisp packets. So far, so predictable.

But where was Teodora?

CHAPTER 9

·

Eddie Sapphire and the Blue Brigade

'Hello-oo?' called Amy, keeping her voice low. 'Teodora? It's me, Amy.'

'What if this is another trap?' said Jesse nervously.

'Yeah. I don't like this,' said Emma.

All around, the gate was silent. I couldn't hear anything at all, not even Freddie and Luke's party zone in the executive lounge. 'Let's wait a few more minutes,' I said. 'Maybe she's scared to come out.'

'Why's this girl so important anyway?' said Boris.

Amy rolled her eyes huffily. 'You know why. Her mother's Caitlin Yang. She was trying to stop Orwell Wells. If anyone knows how to track down the MACE machine, it'll be Teodora.'

'Are you sure? She's a girl. Girls are rubbish at scientific stuff.'

'Quite the reverse,' said Amy. 'I once read a book about the male brain. It was very short indeed.'

Opening her laptop, she checked the message again, just to be sure. 'Gate 28. That's what she said.'

'Maybe Teodora made a mistake,' said Emma. Then her eyes widened. 'Or maybe she isn't here at all. She's just another crazy YouTube prankster, winding you up for a joke.'

That seemed to convince the others. 'All right,' said Boris. 'Let's get out of here.'

'Just a few more minutes,' pleaded Amy.

But Boris was already heading back the way we'd come. Jesse and Emma turned to each other, shrugged, and started to follow him. Then we heard shouts at the end of the corridor and stampeding feet.

'Oh, no,' said Emma. 'It's the slingshot kids. They're coming this way…'

She caught my eye and I realised suddenly that she wanted me to take charge of the situation. For a moment, this puzzled me – I'm really not a natural leader and I hadn't exactly chosen to be responsible for a whole bunch of people. They weren't even my friends. But, then again, I was already responsible for Amy. And Boris – well, Boris definitely wasn't a leader. He was too reckless for that. Emma could have been, but maybe she was too emotional. Jesse was too laid-back, too cautious. Johnny was too young, and he already had his role, driving us all around. So… that really did only leave me. And maybe they all did count as friends, given everything we'd been through so far.

To think all of this took about half a second, though it felt like more. They were all looking at me now, and the footsteps were thundering closer.

'I think they went this way, Mr Sapphire,' a voice shouted.

'Quick,' I said. 'Don't make a sound. Follow me.'

There were two doors leading off Gate 28. One, behind a desk, was the way you walked to the aircraft. The other had a sign saying 'AIRPORT PERSONNEL: NO ENTRY', and in smaller letters beneath it, 'BAGGAGE HANDLING'. It would be locked, I was sure. And – thanks to my trusty Ankylosaurus – I was pretty sure I'd be able to unpick the lock. Quickly I drew my silver dinosaur out of my pocket, ran over to the door and, just as I'd done the previous day at Oakwood Academy, used the spike of wire to fumble with the lock. It took me a few tries before the mechanism slipped and the door swung open. Just in time! Our pursuers were nearly upon us. I bundled Amy through the doorway; Boris, Emma and Jesse pelted through after us. Emma slammed the door and we locked it again – and bolted it too – from the inside.

We all breathed out such massive sighs of relief that it was almost funny.

'Shhh,' said Emma, ear to the door. Our pursuers had reached the gate now. We could hear them, stomping about, muttering to each other. They even tried the handle of the door and rattled it a few times. Then we heard the static-y whistle of a walkie-talkie.

'Mr Sapphire,' said someone. 'Sorry, I mean, Mr Sapphire, sir. Henry here. Bridget and I are at Gate 28. There's no one here. They may have left the airport.'

'Any idea what the intruders were looking for?' came a voice on the other end. It was a very posh voice, a bit like Hugh Grant's in *Paddington 2*. The kind of voice you hear on the radio a lot. The voice was also quite unpleasant. I didn't think we were going to be best friends with its owner, somehow.

'No, sir. They didn't tell Luke and Freddie what they wanted, sir,' said a female voice.

'Luke and Freddie are imbeciles,' said the voice. 'Get back here. We'll regroup. Be vigilant. Keep an eye out for strangers wandering about.'

'Yes, Mr Sapphire, sir.'

'This airport belongs to me now. I can't have anyone coming here and challenging my authority.'

Boris froze. 'Johnny!' he mouthed. 'He's in the car park.'

'Don't panic,' I said. 'Johnny will be fine.'

But secretly I was worried too. Johnny was only eleven, and he was all by himself... We needed to find Teodora and get out of this dreadful place as soon as we possibly could. I looked about. We were in a narrow corridor, with a row of lockers on one side and a stairwell at the end. 'Come on,' I said. 'We may as well go down the stairs. There's no point in heading back to the departures lounge. We'll run into Luke and Freddie, and they may have been joined by reinforcements by now.'

'We can't leave until we've found Teodora,' protested Amy.

'Face it, Amy, she's not here,' said Boris. Then he screamed – or rather, he began to scream and I managed to clap a hand over his mouth to stop most of it from getting out. I felt like screaming too, though, because just ahead of us a locker door was swinging open, very slowly, all by itself...

'Oh my God,' said Jesse. 'The airport is haunted.'

And then a girl – probably about eleven or twelve years old, with tangled dark hair and a red hoodie and blue jeans – jumped down from the locker, where she'd obviously been hiding. She landed neatly on her feet, looking at us with heavy suspicion. Then her eyes fell on Amy. 'I know you,' she said. 'I recognise you from your profile picture. You sent the message.'

'That's right,' said my sister. 'I'm Amy.'

'I'm Teodora. You can call me Teo.'

'You can call me Amy,' said Amy. 'This is my brother Oliver, and these are Emma, Boris and Jesse.'

We all said hi, feeling slightly awkward, as though it was the wedding of some remote cousin and we were stuck at the kids' table being forced to socialise against our will.

'I'm so glad you've come,' said Teodora. 'I was scared, you know, that the MACE machine was going to knock out the internet, the way it did with radio frequencies and mobile phones. Thankfully, though, we're still online. I uploaded that video hoping that someone would find me, and you did. Otherwise I'd have been stuck here for ever.' As she spoke, she was busy pulling bits and pieces – an iPad, juice cartons, energy bars, a teddy bear and a toothbrush – out of the locker and packing up a small rucksack. 'Let's get moving,' she said, sprinting off down the corridor towards the stairs.

'Who is Mr Sapphire?' I said.

'Oh, him,' said Teodora. 'He's completely insane. He's the reason I haven't been able to get out of this wretched airport. He's got scouts all over, looking for intruders... He thinks he owns the place.'

'You mean he wouldn't let you leave?' said Jesse. 'Why?'

'Others have tried,' said Teodora. 'He forced them to join his gang. The Blue Brigade, or something, they're calling themselves. I don't like that kind of thing, and obviously I have better stuff to do than patrol Luton airport all day pretending that I'm its queen. Have you got a car, Oliver?'

'No,' I said. Her shoulders sank. 'But we do have a bus,' I went on, smiling a little.

'A bus! Oh, thank goodness.' She sped up and we followed her. At the bottom of the stairs was a glass door leading out onto the tarmac. Emma shut her eyes reflexively, but I nudged her to open them again because as far as I could see there were no plane wrecks anywhere nearby. There were plenty of planes, though, that had never taken off in the first place without pilots to fly them. I saw EasyJet and Ryanair and Vueling and Wizz Air and some other airlines that I didn't know.

Teodora turned around with a finger over her lips. 'Move as quietly as you can out here,' she said. 'We don't want to get caught. Trust me.'

Out in the open, the air was freezing and frosty and immediately turned Amy's nose pink. I made a mental note to get her some warmer clothing; none of us even had coats. We crept along in the shadow of a gigantic EasyJet plane. I was feeling massively confused about where we were but Teodora seemed to have a better understanding of the geography of the place. She turned again and made frantic hand gestures that I figured meant 'be quiet and follow me' – then she ran in a diagonal line over to another aircraft. I realised that she was taking us across the airfield in as covert a way as possible to avoid detection. Slowly, surely, we were making our way to the other end of the tarmac. I kept Amy close by me at all times.

'OK,' panted Teodora. 'Now we need to sprint across to that door there. It'll take us into baggage reclaim. From there we'll get out of the terminal and go and find your bus. This is the riskiest part, though. I think he's got people watching the CCTV. Ready, guys? One, two, and...'

She set off, almost flying, the sun lighting up her hair as she ran. Here was a proper leader, I thought. Teodora was totally fearless. I grabbed Amy's hand and we sprinted off after Teodora, with Boris, Emma and Jesse following close behind. I was feeling more than a little out of breath as I ran. I've never been that keen on athletics. But we were more or less keeping up with Teodora as we raced towards the door that stood between us and escape.

Then we heard hooting. It was coming from our left, and our right... and behind us too. I snuck a glance to one side and saw one of those baggage-handling trucks zooming towards us, wheels bouncing. It was manned by about six kids in long blue reflective coats, all with sunglasses on. Some of them were armed with slingshots. There was another truck coming from the other direction. And, directly on our tail, was a third.

Teo was the first to get to the door. 'It's locked!' she yelled.

'Oliver, do your lock-thing!' said Emma.

I already had my dinosaur key ring ready in my hand, but I was so sweaty and shaky that I dropped it. By the time I'd picked it up, all three trucks had closed in and several blue-jacketed boys had leapt out and formed a tight circle around us. They didn't look like a gang. They looked like an army.

It was pretty scary stuff.

'Oh, Oliver,' Amy wailed. 'Now how are we going to get to the MACE machine and bring the adults back?'

'Well, well, well,' said a voice. Someone stepped through the line of blue jackets. A tall boy, with straight black hair almost down to his shoulders. He had sunglasses on, and a very sharply cut dark blue suit. Although he was clearly a teenager, he looked a lot like a businessman who doesn't mind stealing people's money.

'I'm Eddie Sapphire,' said the boy. 'This is my airport.' He smiled an enormous smile, as though this was the most exciting thing ever. 'These are my boys. Oh, and girl – sorry, Bridget.'

I saw that one of the army was indeed a girl – a redhead with a rather grumpy expression.

'This isn't your airport,' said Boris.

'But it is,' said Eddie Sapphire, smiling even more widely. 'I've claimed it. I run the place now. With my Blue Brigade.'

The army looked smug.

'And you are my newest recruits!' Eddie Sapphire continued.

'We are not,' I said, as loudly as I could. 'We're leaving.'

The black-haired boy took off his sunglasses. His eyes were bright blue. Like sapphires. He raised an eyebrow thoughtfully.

'Oh, I don't think so,' he said. The smile was nastier now. I got the impression that Eddie Sapphire was about as dangerous a character as I was ever going to meet. He made Dad seem totally harmless by comparison.

'Yes, we are,' said Amy. 'We've got stuff to do.'

'What stuff?'

'None of your business,' said Teodora.

But Bridget suddenly held up a walkie-talkie.

"Scuse me, Mr Sapphire, sir. Think you ought to hear this.' She pressed the PLAYBACK button and we all heard Amy's voice from a few minutes ago:

'Oh, Oliver. Now how are we going to get to the MACE machine and bring the adults back?'

Eddie Sapphire looked genuinely horrified for a second. Then he regained control of his face. Scowling at Amy, he said, 'Bring the adults back? Bring the adults back? Never. I will never allow it.'

'You can't stop us,' said Amy, but her voice was trembling.

'Brigade!' shouted Eddie Sapphire. 'Seize them all!'

And the circle closed in, with big, menacing grins. I could see the six of us reflected in their sunglasses. We looked petrified.

Then something extraordinary happened. Instead of reaching us, one by one they were thrown back as though by some kind of invisible force field. It sent them flying backwards with yells of surprise and outrage. We were standing inside some kind of ring of protection. When he saw what was happening, Eddie Sapphire rolled up his sleeves and dived towards us. But he was thrown back too. 'What is going on here?' he bellowed.

I looked down at Amy, and sure enough, her eyes were closed and her cheeks were shiny with effort.

She was holding them back with her new, incredible powers. But I could see that it was exhausting her.

'I can't... I can't keep this up forever,' she whispered.

The door! Suddenly I realised that we had an escape route just behind us. This time I had no problems with my Ankylosaurus. The lock gave way with a click and we raced through the door. Amy stayed behind just long enough to hold the Blue Brigade off for another few seconds, then Emma swept her away to join us as we charged through baggage reclaim. Behind us we heard angry shouts as the Blue Brigade reassembled themselves and gave chase. I could hear Eddie barking instructions: 'Head round to the front of the terminal. We'll cut them off.'

'He's not going to let us leave,' Emma said, her eyes huge.

'Yes, he is,' said Boris. But I got the impression he was only saying it to cheer her up. We raced past the unmoving carousels while the Blue Brigade charged after us, firing slingshots every few seconds. We dodged the bullets as best we could. Baggage reclaim was massive. I was getting tired; I think we all were, but we were getting nearer to the exit. Then my heart sank. More blue-jacketed recruits were standing in a chain across the exit, with baseball bats in their hands.

Then we head two voices saying: 'Beep beep! Anyone need a lift?'

It was Luke and Freddie, driving alongside us in a special assistance vehicle.

'Yes!' we chorused, piling on board.

'Whoopee!' yelled Freddie, as the vehicle cut a crazy path towards the exit doors. Ahead of us, the Blue Brigade stood firm, maybe hoping that we were going to slow down, but then as it became clear that we weren't going to, they dived out of the way.

'Why are you helping us?' said Jesse. 'You sent us into a trap before. Remember?'

'Oh, but that was ages ago,' said Luke. 'We're bored of this airport now. And we've run out of movies to watch!'

Out through the arrivals hall we rolled, past the empty shops and forgotten trolleys laden with luggage. I could see the road now. A huge fallen aeroplane lay like a beached whale just outside the automatic doors. The car park was just around the corner. I hoped Johnny was still there, waiting for us. Then, to my horror, we began to lose speed.

'What's wrong?' I said.

'Battery's flat!' said Freddie. 'Oh dear, oh dear.'

'We'll run for it,' said Teodora, leaping down as the vehicle ground to a halt. But there, just in front of us, was Eddie Sapphire. With another ten of his soldiers.

'Not so fast,' he said.

'Amy,' I muttered. 'Do something.'

'Like what?' said Amy.

'I dunno. Anything!'

And my incredible little sister thought for a moment and then balled her hands into fists, closed her eyes, and set her mouth in a straight line. At first, I didn't know what was happening. Then I saw that the long white wing of the fallen aircraft was detaching itself slowly from the body of the plane and rising into the air like a giant surfboard. It was almost beautiful to watch. The wing hovered in mid-air, then it started to glide towards us. Eddie's men yelped and leapt out of the way as we scrambled on board the wing.

'You're coming with us, right?' I said to Luke and Freddie. Nodding eagerly, they scrambled on board as well. 'All aboard the Storm-mobile!' I said.

'Lift off!' Amy added, with a grin.

It was pretty amazing. Eddie Sapphire howled in fury as the wing climbed higher into the air – all eight of us clinging on for dear life – and then sailed over the road, high above the security fence, and into the short-stay car park, where Johnny was waiting at the wheel of the 328 bus.

'Hey, guys,' I said, as we landed alongside the bus, giggling with relief and excitement. 'Does anyone mind if we call ourselves Team Storm?'

CHAPTER 10

•

Whipsnade Zoo

So now we were nine in Team Storm. Me, Amy, Boris, Johnny, Jesse, Emma, Teo, Freddie and Luke. To be honest, I wasn't quite sure about the last two. Could we really trust them? They seemed harmless enough, as they made themselves at home at the back of the bus, eating popcorn, talking in weird rhyming verses and occasionally laughing like hyenas at their own jokes. But I couldn't forget that they'd been working for Eddie Sapphire, keeping lookout in the executive lounge. Then again, Luke and Freddie had helped us to escape, showing up with a special assistance vehicle just when we needed it.

Once we were back on the motorway and away from Eddie Sapphire and his Blue Brigade, we all started to relax again. By now, it was late afternoon. The clock on the bus was showing 4.37. I was starving; all I'd eaten all day was snack food.

'Where are we heading?' said Johnny, who was now changing gears as though he'd been driving buses all his life. 'Back to London?'

Teo was sitting next to Emma, across the aisle from me and Amy. Boris was in front with his brother – I got the feeling that he was pretty relieved to be reunited with him. Jesse was having a nap. Teo frowned. 'Not London, no,' she said. 'We need to get to Bristol.'

'How come?' I said.

'That's where I live. Mum's office contains all her notes, all her work. We'll find something there to help us, I'm sure of it.'

'Teodora,' said Emma, in her best schoolteacher voice. 'Will you tell us everything you know about Professor Wells and the MACE project?'

While Boris helped Johnny to navigate, Teo opened a bag of popcorn, put her feet up on the seat in front of her and told us the whole story.

'My mum studied particle physics with Professor Wells when she was younger. They were classmates. He wasn't crazy then, but he was always quite odd, she said. I think he'd had quite an unhappy childhood – he might have grown up in an orphanage, but I'm not totally sure about that. Anyway, one thing that is true is that Orwell Wells hated kids. He couldn't stand to be around them. He and Mum stopped hanging out as he got weirder and weirder, and for a while they didn't see much of each other. Then they met again when they were both doing government research. Wells was trying to design a machine that would use sound waves to transport people to an alternate dimension, Mum said.'

'How does that work?' I said.

'I'm not too sure,' said Teo. 'Something to do with tuning to a precise frequency.'

'So that's what caused the yellow wave?' said Amy.

'Yep,' said Teo.

'What do you mean by an alternate dimension?' said Emma.

'He imagined a parallel universe,' said Teo. 'Something that existed alongside ours, separated by some kind of tiny, invisible barrier, or force. Like gravity, almost.' She shrugged. 'I'm not a scientist, so I don't really know. This is just what Mum told me. Anyway, nobody ever thought that he would succeed. I can't believe he tricked them into letting him do it on national TV. But that was the other thing about Wells – he wanted to be famous. He wanted everyone to know who he was, and how great he was.'

Amy was deep in thought. 'So... his plan worked. His experiment was a success. He hated kids so much that he removed all the adults to an alternate dimension, leaving all the children behind.'

Teo nodded. 'When Mum found out what he was planning to do, she did everything she could to stop him. She went to the TV studio; she broke in just as the experiment was starting. But it was too late. I was at Luton airport with my dad – we'd just arrived back from a skiing trip. I was watching the whole thing on the TV in the arrivals hall. Then – well, you know the rest. A yellow wave, and then nothing. No adults. No mobile phone signal. No radio stations.'

She turned to Amy. 'And one eight-year-old girl who suddenly develops telekinetic powers.'

Jesse woke up with a start as we rolled over a pothole. 'Tele-ki-what now?' he said sleepily.

'Telekinesis,' said Teo, slowing her voice and speaking really clearly. 'Amy can move objects and create force fields with her mind alone. Bet you couldn't do that on Sunday night, right, Amy?'

Amy shook her head. 'So,' she said, 'you reckon the disturbance caused by the MACE machine gave me my powers?'

'I do,' said Teo. 'It's certainly likely.'

'So what can we do?' said Emma. 'To reverse the experiment, I mean.'

'Well,' said Teo, 'Mum kept a record of everything

that Wells was up to in her lab. I reckon if we go through her papers and read her notes, we should find a way to adjust the settings on the machine and bring the adults back again.'

'You think so?' I said.

'I hope so,' said Teo. 'There's only one problem. One big problem, I mean.'

'What's that?' said Amy.

'I don't know where the machine is,' said Teo.

Up ahead, Johnny yawned. 'Guys,' he said. 'It's been a pretty long day. D'you think we could stop somewhere?'

We were just passing a sign for Whipsnade Zoo. Amy and I were huge fans of Whipsnade and had visited many times with Mum and Dad. There would definitely be food there, and hopefully beds of some kind, maybe in those lodge things where you could camp all night with the wildlife.

'Guys,' I said. 'Anyone fancy a little trip to the zoo?'

We were all in favour.

•

Whipsnade is an enormous place – far larger than London Zoo – and even on a busy day, it never seems particularly full, because of the huge distances that you have to walk, or drive. The sun was setting as we drove through the raised barriers by the entry kiosks and parked the bus near the bear enclosure. There were loads of parked cars, but not a soul in sight.

'It's completely deserted,' said Boris, jogging over to the side of the ape enclosure and peering in. I wandered over to join him. A family of chimpanzees was sitting cuddled up on a tree trunk.

'Hey, I wonder if the electricity's still on,' said Emma.

'It is,' said Jesse, nodding at the lamps that were just coming on alongside the high security fences. 'Oh!' he said suddenly. 'The animals! There's been nobody looking after them since Monday morning. I hope they're OK. What have they been eating?'

'Grass and vegetation,' said Boris. 'The usual stuff. They can forage for themselves, can't they?'

'OK for the herbivores,' said Teo, 'but what about the others? The lions and tigers and so on?'

'I dunno,' I said.

'Maybe they're eating each other,' said Luke. 'Do bats eat cats?'

'Do rats eat bats?' said Freddie. Then they both started laughing uproariously.

Emma rolled her eyes. 'Where are we going, Oliver?'

'To get some food,' I said, leading everyone towards the place that I knew used to serve quite delicious wood-fired pizza.

When we got to the River Cottage restaurant, we were surprised to see that it wasn't empty. One long table was occupied by kids ranging from much younger to quite a bit older than us. They were eating pizza and studying giant maps of Whipsnade and talking quietly, not always in English. For a moment it all seemed so normal – apart from the fact that there were no adults – that I forgot the weirdness of the last couple of days completely. All the kids looked up when we came in. Then one of them waved us over – a dark-skinned boy in a green jumper. 'Hey!' he said. 'What are you guys doing here?'

'Long story,' I said as we approached. It was a massive relief to finally encounter some kids who weren't armed with any kind of weapon or strange accessory. Mr Sapphire and his sunglasses-wearing crew were by now, mercifully, a distant memory.

We all introduced ourselves. There were nine of them, too. They were tourists from other countries: France, America, Brazil, Japan, Mexico, Sweden.

'We were visiting the zoo with our families yesterday morning,' said the French girl, Claudine, 'when – poof! – all the adults were gone. We thought it was a magic trick.'

'It was a kind of magic trick,' said Teo.

'Please, have some pizza,' said the dark-skinned boy, whose name was Gael. We all sat down and helped ourselves gratefully. I was glad to see that there was loads of pizza, beautifully cooked, and plenty of juice and Coca-Cola to drink.

'Did you see a tiger wandering around out there?' said the Japanese boy, Minoru.

'A tiger!' said Emma.

'Yes. It escaped when we went to feed it. We've been looking after the animals as best we can, the whole time,' said Gael. 'It's hard, with only nine of us, but we manage.'

'We didn't see any tiger,' I said.

'I wish we had,' said Johnny. 'Tigers are cool.'

'We need to capture it,' said the Mexican girl, Paloma. She was the tallest of all of the kids, with long, dark, curly hair and a lot of goth make-up around her eyes. 'But we are all a little terrified. It's not safe to let it wander around the zoo – not for us, and not for all the other creatures here.'

'We'll help you capture the tiger,' I said, before I'd even had time to think about it properly.

The kids were delighted by this suggestion. I could see they were all exhausted. I didn't know how many zookeepers typically worked in a place like Whipsnade, but probably at least a hundred. These kids were doing everything with no experience or training, and there were only nine of them.

'That would be so kind,' said Gael. 'You must stay in the Lookout Lodges tonight. I think you'll enjoy that.'

'Oh, we will,' I said.

I'd always wanted to stay overnight at Whipsnade Zoo. It was a bit of a dream come true for me, and I could tell that the others were all feeling the same way. The Zoo Tribe (as I had decided to call them) were already occupying five of the huts. We now occupied five more: me and Amy; Emma and Teo; Boris and Johnny; Freddie and Luke. Jesse got one all to himself, which I think he was pretty pleased about. The huts were made of polished wood, and inside there were beds with lovely soft duvets and spare blankets in cupboards and grey sofas. There were books on the shelves and bathrooms with fluffy towels. It was all very comfortable.

'If we didn't have a mission, I'd be happy to spend more time here,' I said, bouncing on my bed. Outside, the trees were waving in the wind, and I could hear, far off, the sounds of animals howling and owls hooting. It was awesome. 'I reckon the Zoo Tribe could use a bit more help, don't you think?'

'Well, we can't stay here,' said Amy, rubbing her eyes. 'We have to get to the MACE machine.'

'I know,' I said.

'Night, Ols.'

'Night, Amy. Sleep tight.'

My little sister climbed into bed and was asleep almost before her head hit the pillow. I watched her sleeping, feeling protective. I wondered if using her new powers was making her tired. I made another mental note, to make sure that she was eating enough every day. Amy shivered a little in her sleep, and I went over and arranged an extra blanket on top of her. All around us, Whipsnade was falling silent, apart from the occasional squeak or rustle. The tiger, wherever he (or she) was, must also have been fast asleep. Not, I hoped, too nearby. I thought I heard the screech of car tyres, somewhere not that far away; for a while, I sat up in bed, listening intently, but soon all was quiet again. I must have imagined it. It was easy, I decided, to get paranoid, now that we were living in a world with no grown-ups. A world where crazy kids could take over airports, attacking anyone who got in their way. Then again, not all kids were crazy. There were the good guys, like the Zoo Tribe, who just wanted to look after the animals at Whipsnade. And us, of course. We were good guys. We wouldn't give up until we'd found a way to reverse the MACE experiment and bring the adults back from this weird alternate dimension that Professor Wells had dragged them all off to. It was a pretty tall order, I kept thinking. Could we manage it, even with Teo to help us? Even with Amy's special powers to get us out of difficulties?

Oh well. We'd have to see. I realised, as I lay there in the dark, that the way I thought about myself was changing. I used to think that I was bad, because of being expelled from Phoenix Feather High. Because Dad treated me like I was bad. I never thought there was anything special about me, anything different. Not any more. Now I was a leader. And a good guy.

The last thing I thought before I drifted off to sleep was something that Mum used to say. 'No matter what happens, tomorrow's another day.'

CHAPTER 11

•

The Tiger

The next morning, we had breakfast early on picnic tables outside the lodges: croissants and baguettes and fruit yogurts that the Zoo Tribe had picked up from the cafeteria. Apparently, the fridges and freezers were well stocked with supplies, just as you'd expect from a major tourist attraction. The Zoo Tribe were in a very good mood. The Mexican girl, Paloma, told us that it was her birthday today. She had added some extra sparkle to her gothic eye make-up.

'How old are you?' asked Jesse.

'Eighteen,' she said.

Amy and Teo looked at each other, frowning. I wondered what their problem was.

'What time of day were you born?' Teo said to Paloma.

She looked surprised, then said, 'Twelve noon.'

I was about to ask Amy privately what they were

worried about when Johnny came jogging up to the breakfast tables. He was out of breath and looked anxious. 'Something really odd has happened,' he said. 'Our bus has been vandalised!'

Emma spread jam on a baguette for him as he told us the story. He'd got up early, apparently, and had gone to the bus to check that it was OK. He felt very protective of it.

'When I got to where we'd parked it, I just had this feeling that there was something wrong,' he said. 'At first, everything looked fine. Nothing had been taken and the keys were still there. But then I looked closer and I realised – the fuel tank had been emptied and all the tyres were flat!'

'That is *so* weird,' said Boris. 'Who would do something like that? It doesn't make any sense.'

I looked from person to person, but the expression on the face of every member of the Zoo Tribe was the same: baffled and upset. I couldn't believe any of them would have vandalised our bus.

'I thought I heard a car,' I said, remembering. 'Late last night.'

We all walked over to the bus to see for ourselves. Sure enough, the tyres had been punctured and the cap of the fuel tank was gone. A dark splash of petrol on the ground showed that someone had managed to drain the entire tank. Perhaps with a hose of some kind. Johnny was almost in tears. 'How on earth are we going to get to Bristol?' he said.

I turned to the Zoo Tribe. 'Did any of you come by car?'

They all shook their heads. 'We came by train,' said Minoru.

Amy was deep in thought. 'There are hundreds of parked cars here,' she said. 'We just need to find the keys. They'll be in handbags or trouser pockets... it'll be hard, though. To find a set of keys to match the right car. Perhaps impossible. We'll just have to try.'

'All right,' I said. 'Let's split up into two groups. I'll go with Gael and anyone else who wants to come to try and locate the tiger. Everyone else can go on a key hunt. Sound good?'

'Yes, Oliver,' they chorused.

As my group climbed into golf carts and rolled away, I couldn't help feeling a tiny bit concerned. I'd never had any dealings with tigers before. The most dangerous animal I'd ever encountered was our neighbour Mrs Willis's sharp-toothed, territorial cat. I didn't want to show that anything was bothering me, though. Not now that I was definitely the leader.

So off we went. Boris and Teo represented Team Storm, plus Gael, Claudine and Paloma. Luke and

Freddie also wanted to come. I think they were excited about seeing a tiger up close. Everyone else stayed behind. There was lots to do at all the different animal enclosures – animals needed to be fed and cages needed to be cleaned. I was kind of amazed at how organised they all were.

'We last saw the tiger at the elephant enclosure,' said Gael, map-reading, as we headed for the Asia section of the park. 'This country is so cold,' he added.

'Well, at least it isn't snowing,' I said.

The elephant enclosure was peaceful. Occasionally, an elephant lumbered by. I admired their wrinkled skin and massive sense of contained power. Sometimes I saw a calf, cuddled up close to its mother. It made me miss Mum. And also, weirdly, Dad. I pictured him stuck in this alternate dimension that Teo had been talking about. If we were living in a world with no adults, then they were living in a world with no kids. Orwell Wells had separated the adults from the children, as cleanly as a knife cutting butter. Watching the elephant mother walking close to her child, I thought for the first time about how totally wrong that was.

'We have to stop this,' I said to Boris.

For a moment he was silent. Then he said, 'Yeah. I know. It was cool at first, but now… everything's just going to break down, isn't it?'

From area to area we went, but in vain. There was no sign of the tiger anywhere. Eventually, Gael said, 'Look, Oliver, we can't hold you up any longer. You have something important to do.'

'We promised we'd help you catch the tiger,' I said.

'No. You guys go on to Bristol. Find out how to bring the adults back. We'll look after everything here.'

'OK,' I said. 'If you're sure.'

But as we drove back to the Lookout Lodges, we saw something that made my blood go cold. Amy was sitting quietly at a picnic table, engrossed in a book. I couldn't see what it was but from the colour of the cover I suspected that it was *The Worst Witch* by Jill Murphy, which is one of Amy's favourite books. There were no other kids anywhere in sight. But – about ten metres away – stood the most enormous tiger I'd ever seen. It was low in the shadows under the trees. Its tail was aloft and its hackles were raised.

'Oh, look!' said Luke gleefully. 'A tiger! Do tigers eat spiders, I wonder?'

'Shut. Up,' I said.

We parked the golf carts and approached, as silently as we could, on foot. Next to me, Gael was taking a tranquilliser gun from a case and fitting it with a dart. I was impressed that he knew what he was doing, but he explained in a whisper that his mother was an animal handler who worked on movie sets. We drew closer and closer. So did the tiger. I could almost hear it thinking: 'Finally! Lunchtime!' Frantically, I thought about what would be the best thing to do. I opened my mouth to yell at the tiger and distract it. But, just then, we heard a clattering from the trees. We looked over. It was Emma, holding a stainless-steel water bottle that she was bashing with a spoon.

'Hey!' she called. 'Over here!'

The tiger turned with a magnificent swish of its tail and began to bound over towards Emma. From its throat came a terrifying roar.

'Emma!' I yelled.

The tiger turned, muscles stiffening. It saw me. Its mouth opened in what was almost a smile. Then it came lumbering towards me. Next to me, Gael raised the tranquilliser gun to shoulder height, preparing to shoot... I closed my eyes.

I opened them again.

Jesse had appeared from one of the huts. He was standing beside the tiger and patting its neck. It was purring at him, every trace of aggression totally gone. 'What a lovely tiger you are,' he said affectionately. 'Beautiful.'

He beckoned us with a wave. 'Don't worry,' he said. 'He won't hurt us.'

Slowly, very slowly, we came closer. 'How... how can you talk to it like that?' I asked.

'Well, I love animals,' said Jesse. 'I've always thought that my cat at home understood what I was saying and vice versa. So when I looked out of the lodge window and saw the tiger going for you guys, I just came out and sent it a kind of thought-wave – it's really hard to explain – and it saw me, and I held out my hand, and it came slinking over to me. I asked him what he wanted and he said that he's very hungry and just wants to get back to his enclosure. Poor thing.'

'Wow,' I said, as Amy and Teo went up to pet the tiger, and Claudine and Minoru offered it a drink of water. We were all massively impressed that Jesse could communicate in a way that animals understood. It seemed that Amy wasn't the only one with special powers. Maybe, just maybe – I found myself thinking – we all had things inside us that made us special.

We just needed to find out what they were.

·

The tiger became extremely attached to Jesse and followed him around for the next hour or so, while we looked all over Whipsnade for some car keys that would actually operate one of the parked cars. It was like the world's most frustrating Easter egg hunt.

'This is hopeless,' said Emma at last.

Johnny was looking longingly at a parked Aston Martin. 'I guess so,' he said, kicking some gravel. The tiger made sympathetic noises. The sky made noises of a different kind: with a grumble of thunder, it suddenly began to rain.

Everyone was looking at me again, so I made a leadership decision. 'Let's have some pizza,' I said.

So we went out of the rain and back to the restaurant and a couple of Zoo Tribe kids fired up the oven and pretty soon we were all – tiger included – munching on thin crust pizza with scrumptious toppings. The only people who weren't there were Luke and Freddie, who had gone off in a golf cart to explore the zoo and see if they could find any DVDs.

Gael raised his paper cup of Coca-Cola. 'It's nearly twelve o'clock,' he said. 'Happy birthday, Paloma!'

'Happy birthday,' we chorused. It was genuinely nice, in this crazy, mixed-up world, to have a moment of celebration. Paloma laughed so much that some of her black eye make-up smudged. Full of pizza, the tiger had fallen asleep in a corner of the restaurant and every minute or so snored in a growly sort of way.

'Ah, thank you, friends,' she said. 'I never thought I'd be spending my birthday at the zoo…'

She stopped, her mouth open in surprise. I automatically looked all around to see what new evil was approaching. But we were alone in the restaurant.

'Oh my God,' said Emma. 'What's going on?'

Paloma was disintegrating in front of us. It was like a computer game or something. It was like she wasn't real, just made up of pixels. First the ends of her fingers were gone, then her hands... the snake-like ends of her dark, curly hair... her ears... Most of us were screaming. Only Teo and Amy sat solemnly at the table, watching Paloma disappear. By twelve o'clock, she had vanished. It was awful. None of us could believe it. I hugged Amy. Boris hugged Johnny. Jesse hugged the tiger. The Zoo Tribe were pale with shock, many of them crying.

'What just happened?' said Gael finally.

'She turned eighteen,' said Teo in a small voice. 'That's what happened.'

'Oh no,' moaned Emma. 'That's so terrible. But... has she gone to the other dimension, where the adults are? Or has she just... gone?'

Teo shook her head. 'I don't know.' Then she got up, pushing her chair back forcefully. 'We've got to get moving. We can't let this happen to more kids. There could be hundreds – thousands – all over the country, about to turn eighteen... We've got to get to my house in Bristol. I don't care if we have to walk there.'

'It's OK,' I said. 'We get it. We're coming. There must be a car we can drive.'

'If only someone hadn't vandalised our bus,' moaned Johnny for the millionth time.

'Oh, stop complaining about your bus!' snapped Claudine.

'For all we know, you might have been the one who wrecked it,' he snapped back.

'And why would I do that?' she said.

'How should I know?'

'Hey, stop arguing…' said Emma.

Then a shadow fell at the restaurant door and we all stopped talking and looked up, startled.

'Well, well, well, if it isn't my favourite do-gooders,' said a horribly familiar voice.

It was Eddie Sapphire and his Blue Brigade.

CHAPTER 12

•

The Rhinos

Dumbfounded, we stared at the self-proclaimed King of Luton Airport and his band of blue-suited henchmen (and woman). How had he found us? It didn't make any sense.

'I suppose you're wondering how we knew you were here,' said Eddie, smiling broadly. He'd brought about twelve of his Brigade with him. They stood on each side of their leader like well-trained bodyguards. They were all wearing sunglasses even though it was a cold, grey day. It should have looked ridiculous. Instead, it was faintly terrifying.

'You followed us from Luton,' said Emma, in her cross schoolteacher voice.

'Yes, indeed. A red London bus on the motorway... you weren't hard to follow. Not when Henry and Bridget here are such competent drivers.'

Henry and Bridget looked momentarily smug.

So that's why I'd heard the screech of car tyres in the car park last night, I thought. Because they'd followed us.

'Why?' said Jesse. 'We don't care about your airport. We left you alone. Why bother us now?'

'Oh, but isn't it obvious?' said Eddie Sapphire, strolling casually towards the table and helping himself to a slice of artichoke pizza. 'Mmm, delicious pizza. My compliments to the chef.'

'You were saying,' said Boris, his arms folded across his chest.

'Oh yes. Sorry. The fact is, my friends: I can't allow you to "bring the adults back", as you so charmingly put it. Because the world is a far better place without them. So we're here today to put a stop to your crusade, one way or another. We punctured the wheels of your beloved bus and drained the fuel tank, but something tells me that we need to do something a little more... drastic. Brigade, if you please.'

The Blue Brigade advanced on us, slowly but surely, with menacing grins on their faces. And nets in their hands.

'Those are from the zookeepers' storeroom!' hissed Gael. 'They're elephant nets.' He strode forward and came to face the Blue Brigade. Minoru, Claudine and the rest of the Zoo Tribe followed him, all with frowns on their faces. They stood in a row, protecting Team Storm.

'How very sweet!' exclaimed Eddie Sapphire. 'Oliver, I hadn't realised you were such a popular chap. Oh well, we'll just have to capture all of you.'

He whistled – a short sharp burst – and at once the Brigade threw a net over four of the Zoo Tribe. It made a heavy, flapping sound as it fell. Then, perfectly synchronised, they did the same to the other four... I turned to Amy, who was right next to me. She was holding her hands out in front of her but I couldn't see any kind of force field or beam of power or anything like that. Her face was bright pink and she looked exhausted. 'Oh Oliver,' she said. 'I'm trying to do something... There's just too many of them... I can't lift the nets...'

'And now for the rest!' said Eddie Sapphire. The Blue Brigade grinned. They stepped over the captured Zoo Tribe and came towards us with more elephant nets in their hands. I knew I needed to do something, but I just didn't know what to do. I didn't have powers like Amy. My silver Ankylosaurus wasn't going to be any help to me now... Desperately, I stepped forward, raised my arm with my hand scrunched into a fist and punched Eddie Sapphire in the face. It was a good, solid blow, perfectly aimed. It knocked him off balance and he nearly fell over altogether before two of his henchmen came to his rescue.

'Oh dear,' said Eddie Sapphire, reaching forward and grabbing my collar with a strange, sinister smile. 'I don't think you should have done that. You may come to regret it.'

The elephant nets came closer. We were backed up against the restaurant wall: me, Amy, Emma, Teo, Jesse, Boris and Johnny. They had plenty of ridiculously tough-looking nets and we had nowhere to go. I looked at the faces of Team Storm and thought that I'd never seen us all look quite as scared and quite as defeated as we did now...

Then Jesse threw his head back and made a high-pitched sound like a fox.

Rrraaaaaaaaaahhhh!

The sound seemed to come from nowhere. All at once a burst of black and orange lit up the room like a giant wasp as the tiger uncoiled itself from the corner and streaked across the floor. It sent the Blue Brigade flying with two swipes of its huge paws. Its jaws were terrifyingly wide. It seized Eddie Sapphire by his collar and shook him from side to side as though he were nothing more than a troublesome cub. They were all screaming in surprise and horror. From under the nets, the Zoo Tribe were laughing, relieved and disbelieving. One by one, the Blue Brigade scrambled up and were out of the door quicker than Olympic sprinters. Meanwhile, Emma and Johnny knelt down and released the Zoo Tribe from the elephant nets.

Eddie Sapphire was still dangling helplessly from the tiger's jaws. The tiger looked over at Jesse as if to say: 'May I eat this one?'

Jesse paused and then shook his head. 'You've had lots of pizza already,' he said kindly. 'Let him go.' He frowned at Eddie Sapphire. 'Don't come after us again, though. D'you understand?'

But Eddie Sapphire was already gone in a flash of blue suit. We all hugged each other, checking that nobody was hurt, and petted the tiger. Emma put her arms around me and gave me a kiss on the cheek, which delighted me. 'Ordinarily,' she said, 'I don't approve of hitting people, but he really had it coming.'

'Yeah!' said Johnny. 'That guy ruined our bus.'

'Which reminds me,' I said, 'we still don't have a way to get to Bristol.'

Teo went over to the window, looking out at the rain. 'I think I hear engines out there,' she said. 'They've taken their vans and driven away.'

'Good riddance,' said Emma.

Squinting, Teo rubbed a circle in the condensation

on the window. 'It's so hard to see anything out there, but I think… What are those things?'

'Oh, please don't let it be the Blue Brigade coming back again,' said Amy. She was shaking all over, I realised. I wondered if it had scared her, not being able to use her powers to rescue us. But she'd done so much already – lifting aeroplane wings, creating force fields, moving objects – it sort of made sense to me that she'd be getting tired now. Nobody has unlimited power to do anything, do they? I patted her on the arm. 'It's all right, Amy,' I said. 'They've gone. We won't see them again.'

Joining Teo at the window, I looked out at the rain-streaked zoo. 'It's Luke and Freddie,' said Emma. 'But what are they riding? Horses?'

'Unicorns,' said Boris.

Gael said, 'Those are greater one-horned rhinos. The second-largest species of rhinoceros.'

We all ran out of the restaurant into the rain and saw them approaching, one on each rhino. The rhinos were huge. They looked like wrinkly grey armoured tanks, their movements slow but sure and incredibly powerful.

'Those guys are so weird,' said a member of the Zoo Tribe, accurately putting into words what we all thought about Luke and Freddie.

'Hey guys,' said Luke, looking rather small on

the back of the enormous creature. 'Why did the rhino cross the road?'

'Now isn't the time for jokes,' said Teo. 'We need to get to Bristol.'

'Exactly!' said Freddie. 'Why did the rhino cross the road? Because he needed to get to Bristol!'

As usual, they collapsed into hysterical laughter. They were laughing so much it looked like they were going to fall off the backs of the rhinos. Amy was looking very thoughtful. She whispered something to Teo, who whispered back. 'It's an idea,' he said, and then louder, 'Do you think you can?'

'Only one way to find out,' said Amy. And she walked up to one of the rhinos and put a hand on its neck. She stood totally still. So did the rhino. On its back, Freddie froze, looking down at Amy. I could feel a kind of energy in the air as Amy murmured something very softly. The rhino snorted a couple of times and pawed the ground with one hoof. Then its grey, wrinkly skin started to turn black, all around Amy's hand, and the blackness spread outward, all over the animal's neck and head and then across the rest of its body and down its legs until it looked as though it had been carved from a huge piece of black marble. Its eyes glowed red. It was amazing and petrifying in equal measure.

'Wow,' whispered Boris.

'Amy, what are you doing?' I asked.

'Oh, you'll see,' she said.

Now little lumps were sprouting on the rhino's shoulders, like miniature tree stumps. And from the little lumps came forth what looked like black, sprigged trees, that grew and grew until we could see what they were. Silky and dark and beautiful.

'Wings!' exclaimed Emma, in awe.

The rhinoceros looked totally thrilled with its new appearance. It reared up onto its hind legs as Freddie clung on delightedly. Then it gathered itself like a spring, leapt into the air and flew in a triumphant circle over our heads.

'Ya-hooo!' shrieked Freddie.

Without saying a word, Amy moved over to the other rhino. This time it was quicker. Suddenly there we were, on the hill outside the restaurant, as two red-eyed, black-winged rhinos flew around in the sky above us, snorting cheerfully as though they'd been flying all their lives. After a few minutes, they flew down and landed on the ground beside us. Luke and Freddie looked slightly green in the face, but happier than I'd ever seen them.

'Team Storm,' said Amy, also looking happier again now that she'd been able to put her powers to good use, 'I believe we have some transportation to

Bristol. Johnny and Boris, do you think you can figure out a route for us to follow?'

So Johnny and Boris sat down on the grass and with the help of the Great Britain road atlas drew basic directions from Whipsnade to Bristol on some paper napkins. Then Johnny climbed up with Luke and was joined by me, Amy and Emma, while Boris, Teo and Jesse climbed up onto Freddie's rhino.

'Goodbye!' we called to the Zoo Tribe. 'And good luck!'

They echoed this right back at us as they stood there with the tiger on the hill.

'What a nice group of young people,' said Emma. 'They'll be welcome at my Holiday Inn any time. Oh, I do miss it so much. And I miss my mum.'

'It's OK, Emma,' said Amy. 'We'll see all our parents soon enough.'

It was a sensation that I'd never felt before in my life as our rhino gathered speed and then took off, rising up and up into the cold February air. The Zoo Tribe got smaller and smaller and finally we could no longer see them. What an amazing thing the rhino was, I thought. Its wings were like bat wings, just two hundred times bigger. The creature was so huge and nubbly-skinned that it was actually quite comfortable on board. There were plenty of leathery folds to hang on to. I made sure that I was holding Amy tight, though. I didn't want anything to happen to my little sister.

'Next stop, BRISTOL!' I said.

I couldn't resist looking down as we rose higher, leaving the zoo behind, and then higher still. The roads became narrow threads. I scanned them for movement, for the camper vans belonging to Eddie Sapphire and his Brigade. But I didn't see them. The likelihood was that we'd seen the last of the self-proclaimed King of Luton Airport.

'So, Oliver,' said Emma, 'when this is all over, what do you intend to do with your life?'

I was just giving some serious thought to this question when Johnny said cheerfully: 'Oh, don't worry about that. When we bring the adults back, we'll be famous!'

·

CHAPTER 13

The Teodora File

I'd never asked myself how long it might take to cross the country on the back of a gigantic, jet-black, bat-winged rhino, but the answer was: quicker than I might have thought. They were super-powerful, those rhinos, as they dived and glided and hovered twenty or thirty metres above ground level. Whipsnade grew smaller and smaller and then became non-existent. Looking down, I saw frost-covered fields and silent motorways. From the gleeful screams in the air all around, I could tell that the rest of Team Storm was also pretty keen on flying rhinos.

'This is amazing!' screamed Emma several times, her hair streaming out like ribbons behind her.

Only Johnny could from time to time be heard muttering about 'the benefits of driving'. But he seemed happy enough helping Luke with the navigation. The true revelation, however, was Boris. I couldn't believe that only two days ago he had been telling me how stupid he was; how he couldn't read well at all. It seemed like there was no map that Boris couldn't understand. And now he'd actually made one for us, and it was taking us through the air to Bristol.

The only problem with being high up in the sky was the freezing cold. By the time the rhinos began to descend, expertly steered by Luke and Freddie, there wasn't a single one of us who wasn't sneezing and sniffling. It was late afternoon – not yet dark, but getting that way.

Whomp!

With a huge thud, our rhino came to land on a big patch of grass. Then, with another huge thud, the second rhino came down alongside ours. One by one, Team Storm slithered off the rhinos' backs, teeth chattering, rubbing our hands together, hopping up and down to get warm.

'We made it!' said Boris, high-fiving his little brother. 'Great map-work, bro.'

'Do rhinos wear chinos?' asked Freddie.

I looked around. We were in a quiet residential street. On one side was a neat square of grass, where we'd landed, with a playground and a few benches and rose bushes and things. On the other side was a row of houses, some red-brick and others painted pale pink or pale yellow. Teo pointed to a tall, thin, red-brick house right in the middle of the street.

'That's where I live,' she said.

An hour later, we were huddled around the wood-burning stove in Teo's nice warm living room. It felt like forever since I'd been in an actual home, instead of a school or a hotel or a zoo or one of many moving vehicles. We'd eaten a variety of things from Teo's freezer (ice cream, microwaveable cottage pie, and so on) and were well wrapped up in as many jumpers as Teo could find in her cupboards. The rhinos were grazing cheerfully in Teo's tiny back garden. I hoped her mum wouldn't mind that all the geraniums had been consumed, along with most of her herbaceous border.

'This is lovely,' said Emma, curled up in an armchair.

And it was. There was a cosiness to the place that I hadn't experienced since Mum had died. All over the walls were pictures of Teo and her mum. I wondered where Teo's dad was. He didn't seem to be around. Freddie and Luke were fast asleep on the floor – not surprising, since they'd piloted the rhinoceroses all afternoon. Boris and Johnny were playing computer games upstairs. Jesse was doing the washing-up in the kitchen. Amy was sitting on the sofa reading *A Brief History of Time*. Once in a while, her eyelids fluttered down and she'd begin to drift off to sleep. Then she'd sit up, shake her head and carry on reading. I yawned. I was suddenly feeling really tired.

'We could stay here,' said Emma hopefully. 'Just for the night. On beds and sofas.'

I looked at the clock on the mantelpiece. 7pm. The combination of the food in our stomachs, the warmth of the fire and the thought of lovely, comfortable bedding was almost too much... But I was the leader. I needed to carry on leading, no matter how tempting it was to fall asleep.

'Let's see what we can find out about the MACE machine first,' I said. 'Then decide. I don't like the idea of Eddie Sapphire tracking us down again.'

'He doesn't know where we are now, surely,' said Emma.

'Didn't one of us say we were heading to Bristol?' muttered Amy.

'Really?' I said.

'Yeah,' she said. 'I think you might have done, actually, Oliver.'

'Right,' said Teo, jumping off her beanbag. 'Come on, guys. Anything important in the house is kept in Mum's study.'

•

Teo had one of those houses with several floors and narrow, twisty stairs and only a few rooms on each floor. Dr Yang's study was right at the top of the stairs, in the attic. It wasn't locked. Teo opened the door and we stepped in, taking in the piles of books all over the floor, the overstuffed filing cabinet, the loose papers on the rug, the computer with post-it notes stuck all over it...

And a boy with black hair and glasses, dressed in the nerdiest way possible, sitting at the computer. He had on a knitted green sleeveless jumper over a yellow checked shirt, a spotty bow tie, brown tweed trousers and the kind of shoes that people wear to go bowling. He swung round as we entered and screamed. Teo screamed too. Then she said, 'Erwin! What are you doing here?'

The boy stopped screaming and stood up. He must have been sixteen or seventeen years old. He couldn't have been Teo's brother. She'd have told us if she had a brother. Also, he looked nothing like Teo.

'Hey, Teo,' he said. 'Sorry, you scared me. What do you think I'm doing? Same thing you are.'

'How did you even get into my house?'

He looked ashamed. 'I'm afraid I broke a window in the downstairs bathroom. My apologies. I knew Dr Yang had worked with Professor Wells and I figured if anyone knew how to operate the MACE machine, it'd be her. Also, she asked me to look out for you, Teo, if anything ever happened. I thought it was strange at the time. But then the adults disappeared on Monday morning and I decided it would be good to try and find you, if I could.'

Then he looked at me and Amy and stuck out his hand. 'Erwin J. R. Phillips,' he said. He really was the nerdiest person I'd ever seen. But there was something quite impressive about him. Maybe it was the assured way he spoke.

Teo explained: 'Erwin was doing work experience at Mum's lab over half term. He's really into science.'

'Aren't we all?' said Erwin, with a knowing smile. Then he looked puzzled. 'But try as I might, I simply can't log into Dr Yang's computer.'

Teo sat down at the keyboard and typed a username and a password; at once, the screen saver shifted and dissolved and soon we were staring at a desktop full of tidily labelled folders. 'There you go,' she said. We all crowded round the computer, trying not to knock anything over. It really was the fullest study I'd ever seen. I could barely stand up straight, the ceiling was so slanting and low. Teo was clicking on each folder in turn and muttering to herself. 'Research... Shopping... Teaching... Tennis Lessons,' she read out in alphabetical order.

'Look,' said Amy. 'How about this one? It's called Teodora.'

'Oh, that'll just be full of my school reports and baby pictures and stuff,' said Teo. She pulled up a search window and typed in MACE MACHINE, ORWELL WELLS, and various other combinations of things. But nothing came up.

'Try the Teodora file,' urged Amy.

'But I don't have anything to do with the MACE machine,' said Teo.

'Yes, but look – if your mum was going to hide anything she didn't want to be found, I bet she'd put it somewhere that was important to her,' said Amy.

'She's right,' said Emma. 'My mum always uses my name in passwords and stuff like that.'

Teo shrugged. 'OK,' she said. She opened the folder. It was full of sub-folders, again, all labelled. I could've figured out the whole of Teo's life just by reading through them all. Clubs, Letters, Schools… Teo's fingers flew over the keyboard as she opened file after file at random. Then she turned around. 'There's nothing special here,' she said.

Amy pointed. 'What about that, there?' she said.

'That's just a video file,' said Teo.

'But look at the date and time. 12th February 2018, 6.02am,' said Amy, getting more and more excited.

148

'So?'

'That's Monday morning. About three hours before Professor Wells pressed the button and the yellow wave hit and the adults disappeared,' said Erwin.

Teo's eyes grew wide. 'Oh-h-h,' she said. 'Of course.'

Then she froze as the thumping sound of people on the stairs suddenly filled the attic study. The door flew open and Jesse, Boris, Johnny, Freddie and Luke came piling in. 'What's going on?' said Boris. 'Who's this guy?'

'Erwin J. R. Phillips, Junior Scientist of the Year 2017,' said Erwin.

'Everything all right, guys?' I said.

'Yeah, I guess,' said Jesse. 'We wondered what you were up to. Also, we found a smashed window downstairs and we sort of panicked. Thought you might've all been kidnapped by the Blue Brigade.'

'The smashed window was, unfortunately, my doing,' said Erwin. 'What's the Blue Brigade?'

'Just some crazy kids who've been following us since Luton Airport,' said Johnny. 'They wrecked our bus,' he added darkly.

'Sounds like the Golf Club,' said Erwin, straightening his bow tie. 'A bunch of wild, disorderly children who believe that... But never mind. They won't find you here. Let's watch this video, Teodora.'

She clicked on the file and pressed PLAY. At once, the screen was filled with a shot of the very room we were in now. A woman with long, dark hair, who looked a lot like Teo, was sitting at the computer. She was facing the camera and looked very serious indeed.

'Teo, my love,' she said. 'If you're watching this now... well, it means that I've failed. I've failed everyone.'

The woman on the screen blinked, as though to stop herself from crying. Then she carried on, 'I've always known Orwell was planning something. I just didn't know what, or when, or where... Then, by a stroke of luck, another colleague told me that Wells was booked to do a special scientific broadcast, scheduled for 9am today on BBC1. I'm trying to find out where the filming is going to take place, because if I can't find it, then I won't be able to stop it... Wells is pretending that he's invented some kind of incredible machine that combats toxic exhaust fumes, or something. Mathematicians Against Carbon Emissions – that's what he's calling his project. But I know the truth. I know what MACE really stands for.'

There was a pause. There were ten of us crammed into that tiny, book-filled study, and I swear you could have heard a pin drop, it was so quiet.

Teo's mother whispered, 'The Major Adult–Child Experiment. That's what it stands for. A world divided into two separate parallel planes, adults in one place and children in another. That's what he wanted. Crazy, but it's true. And he's a good inventor: an amazing scientist, in his way. He's doing something with sound waves and subatomic particles and colour theory… There's a chance that this machine could actually work.'

She shivered. 'Teo, darling, I'm doing everything I can to track him down. If I can stop him in time… but let's say that I can't. Let's say he's succeeded. You're watching this now. I hope you're not too scared. I hope you're not alone.'

At this, we all looked at each other briefly. Teo definitely wasn't alone. We were all in this together.

'So listen,' said Teo's mum. 'You're going to have to find the MACE machine and reverse the experiment. I wish I knew how it works. The settings will need to be changed, somehow. Look in my filing cabinet. You should find a printout of everything I've managed to find out about the MACE machine, and everything I know about Professor Wells. It's not much, but I hope it helps. The most important thing you need to know, however, is this: Wells built a seventy-two-hour auto-destruct function into the machine. Time is very, very short.'

'What does that mean?' said Boris.

Erwin turned to him. 'It means that the machine

will self-destruct three days after it's activated.'

'What?' said Jesse. 'But... in that case, we only have until just after 9am tomorrow morning!'

'Oh my God,' said Emma, looking green. 'So if we can't find the machine and change the settings before tomorrow morning, the adults will never come back...'

There was silence while we all considered this. A world with no adults. No teachers, doctors, bus drivers, pilots, government officials. No scientists, writers, artists, farmers. No chefs, road-workers, house-builders, zookeepers. Just us. Could we manage to survive? Could we teach ourselves how to do adult jobs, the way the Zoo Tribe had done? The way Johnny did when he proved himself able to drive pretty much anything? Maybe, I thought. With good leadership. Maybe we could. But then, there were kids like Eddie Sapphire, who weren't interested in anything except power. There were the savage-looking kids dressed as wolves. There were kids who would want to work together to make the world a better place, and kids who wouldn't... And the worst of it was, that in this new, strange dimension that Wells had somehow created, each of us, on our eighteenth birthday, would just disappear, bit by bit, the way Paloma had done earlier today.

It didn't bear thinking about any longer.

'Good luck, darling,' said Teo's mother.

The video stopped there.

I stood up and immediately banged my head on a rafter. 'We're going to find that machine if it's the last thing we do,' I said, rubbing my head. Going over to Dr Yang's filing cabinet, I opened the top drawer and began leafing through the identical dark green files. 'What's the time now?' I asked.

'9pm,' said Jesse.

'Right,' I said. 'Here's what we're going to do. Jesse and Emma, please sort out some packing for us – if that's OK with Teo, of course?' I looked over at Teo; she nodded. I went on: 'It looks like it's going to get super-cold tonight and the last thing we want is anyone getting sick. Woolly hats, scarves, torches, cereal bars – pack up whatever you can. Boris and Johnny, can you please tidy up, especially the kitchen. I don't want to leave Dr Yang's house looking like a pigsty. Freddie and Luke, can you go down to the garden and check on the rhinos? See if they need some food and water before we head off.'

'Um,' said Teo. 'Head off where, exactly? We don't know where the MACE machine is.'

'I'm just coming to that,' I said. 'The rest of us – that is to say, me, Amy, Teo and Erwin – are going to find the file and try and figure out where we need to go.' Then I put down the file I was holding and clapped my hands together with great authority. 'Let's get moving, guys!'

And everyone, quite amazingly, went off to follow my directions. Not a grumble. I could hardly believe it. I got to work, sifting through the files in Dr Yang's filing cabinet with the others. Leadership, I thought. It came with certain responsibilities, but I decided that I could definitely get used to it.

CHAPTER 14

•

The Wolf Gang and the Golf Club

The study clock was ticking ominously, as though to remind us that time was running out. All Dr Yang's dark-green files were spread out on the floor. None of them suggested that they contained anything about the MACE machine.

'This is hopeless,' said Teo.

'It does seem, as you say, to be a hopeless situation,' said Erwin. 'But your mother said that the file was there. We have no reason to think she wasn't telling the truth...'

Just as he was saying this, Teo pounced. 'There it is!' she said, seizing a file with some random numbers – 1984 – scribbled on the label in Biro.

I couldn't understand what 1984 had to do with anything.

'George Orwell wrote the book *1984*,' said Teo. 'George Orwell = Orwell Wells. Mum loves puzzles.

Also, she probably didn't want the file to be too obvious in case the wrong people came looking for it.'

The file contained a single, battered document. It was a printout of a biography of Orwell Wells. Teodora's mum had added some notes to it about the MACE machine. There were half-finished questions and scientific equations scribbled all over the document in pencil.

I peered at the document, trying to decipher Dr Yang's writing.

'Wells must be planning something big,' read the document. 'Bigger than anyone believes possible. Why is Wells so interested in coloured light?'

It didn't mean anything to me.

Amy, Teo and Erwin bent their heads low over the documents, talking in whispers. I decided to leave them to it. Science was definitely not my strong point.

As I was making my way downstairs to see how the rest of Team Storm was getting on, Freddie and Luke came barrelling up the stairs, arms waving wildly, and nearly knocked me down.

'What's wrong?' I asked.

'The rhinos have gone!' they wailed. 'They must have flown off!'

Peering out of the landing window, I could see that Luke and Freddie weren't, for once, talking nonsense.

The little garden was empty. Only some broken plant pots showed that large, hungry animals had once been there, stomping about and shredding leaves.

'This is a disaster,' said Freddie. 'A calamity.'

'Or should that be calamari?' added Luke.

I thought about the situation. I'd been counting on using the rhinos to travel to our next destination. It was indeed highly inconvenient. But it wasn't Luke and Freddie's fault, and I told them so. 'Don't worry,' I said. 'We'll work something out.'

Downstairs, Boris and Johnny had tidied up beautifully, just as I'd asked. Emma and Jesse had assembled some holdalls stuffed with useful supplies. Everyone was wearing an extra layer or two. I felt terrible; I was about to give them the disappointing news that we had no transport. Or a destination to aim for.

'Here,' said Emma, handing me a yellow coat. 'Put this on. We're all packed up and ready to go.'

'That's great,' I said. 'The only problem is... well, two problems actually...'

I explained.

Emma's face fell. 'Oh, Oliver. What are we going to do? If we don't even know where we're going...'

'Yes, we do!'

It was Amy, Teo and Erwin, breathless from the

stairs, waving a piece of A4 paper in front of them triumphantly.

'Orwell Wells was a visiting professor at Christ Church College, Oxford,' said Teo. 'He had his own laboratory there. I bet you anything he developed his MACE machine there, on the college grounds. He'd have had total privacy. He could have got the camera crews to go there for the filming.'

'But we need to be sure,' said Jesse. 'This is our last chance. We can't go off in the wrong direction.'

Teo grabbed a bashed-up iPad from the bookshelf. 'This is Mum's old one,' she said. 'Let's see... Here we go.' She pulled up the YouTube video that she herself had posted a few days before. We watched again as Orwell Wells made his claims about global warming, sniggering at the camera... We watched as Caitlin Yang burst in and threw herself at Professor Wells... but this time, instead of looking at the action unfolding in the centre of the room, we scanned the video for anything that would help us locate the machine itself.

'There!' said Erwin. 'Pause it, Teo.'

She paused the video. We all stared at the screen. The room had dark wooden panels on the walls and a single arched window. Through it, you could see greenery. A park of some kind. And beyond it, beautiful, dark-red buildings. A single spire against cloudy skies.

'That's Oxford,' said Erwin. 'Definitely. I did an Accelerated Learning Course for Astonishingly Gifted Children there.'

'We agree,' said Luke and Freddie. 'Oxford is the home of Alice in Wonderland. We've visited the place where Charles Dodgson – otherwise known as Lewis Carroll – wrote his masterpiece, many times. We know the architecture well.'

I noticed that, when they wanted to, Freddie and Luke were truly capable of complete sentences.

'Awesome,' I said. 'Well done, team. At least we do know where we're going.'

We shouldered the bags and put on hats and scarves. 'Let's head for the main bus and coach station,' said Teo, turning off the lights. 'It's only about twenty minutes from here. We may get lucky and find a bus with keys in the ignition.'

'Cool,' said Johnny, running ahead to the door. Boris followed him, carrying a brand-new Great Britain road atlas (borrowed from Teo's house) under his arm like a lucky mascot. Erwin had the file on Professor Wells. Emma, Amy and Jesse were carrying extra bags of supplies. Luke and Freddie seemed to each have a tennis racket but I didn't want to ask why in case I got drawn into another of their weird conversations. Teo and I went last so that Teo could lock up her house.

Then we walked down the short path that led to the front gate and onto the road. It was pitch black and freezing cold; there was no sign of anybody anywhere, which I decided was a good thing. Burying our hands in our pockets, we walked in pairs down the pavement, keeping to long patches of shadow.

'So, Erwin,' I said, 'you mentioned some kind of gang here in Bristol.'

He gulped and nodded. 'There are a few different gangs. The Farming Army. They're okay. They just want to grow runner beans and stuff. The Looters in Suits. They like to break shop windows. But the biggest one by far is the Golf Club. You can guess how they arm themselves.'

'With baseball bats?' said Luke.

'With dead fish?' said Freddie.

Erwin gave them a look.

'I would imagine,' said Amy, who is always serious about this kind of thing, 'that they use golf clubs.'

'Indeed,' said Erwin.

'What do they want?' said Jesse. 'Or do they just want to smash things up too?'

'They think that aliens kidnapped our parents and we need to form an army in order to do battle when they return,' said Erwin with a tight-lipped smile. 'I, of course, did not want to join their gang, which was partly why I went and hid in Dr Yang's house.'

'What about your own house?' said Boris.

'My parents live in Washington, D.C.,' said Erwin. 'I'm here on a study abroad programme.'

After that, it was almost too cold to talk, so we stayed quiet, making our way to the coach station. We crossed a wide road and then came to a park. Here, Teo stopped. 'It's quicker to walk through here,' she said. 'It's usually locked at night.'

'I don't know,' said Erwin. 'They're very quiet, the Golf Club. Stealthy.'

Emma shivered. 'Let's go around,' she said.

'But what are the chances of anyone being in the park?' said Johnny.

'We're in a hurry,' said Amy. 'We only have a few hours before the MACE machine self-destructs. I say let's go for it.'

That seemed to decide everyone and we set off into the park. It was even darker now. I kept hold of Amy's hand, which I could tell was annoying her, but I didn't care. I didn't want to lose her now. I didn't want to lose anyone. We kept to a fast walk, stepping over the usual huddles of long-forgotten adult clothing.

'It's raining,' said Emma.

'No, it's not,' said Jesse. 'It's snowing! Just a little.'

I tilted my face skyward and felt it: the first icy flakes on the tip of my nose. Mum loved snow. She'd always be the first to drag us outside to build some kind of magnificent snow sculpture – never just a snowman, always something more dramatic, like a pyramid, or a three-headed giant. We'd play until it grew dark and then we'd go indoors for as much hot chocolate as we could drink. Sometimes – just sometimes – Dad would come out and play too.

'Mum loved the snow,' said Amy, as though she could hear my thoughts.

'Freddie,' said Luke. 'Why is snow like a snooker table?'

Just then we heard a high-pitched, terrifying cry from a nearby street.

'Oh my God, what was that?' said Emma.

'Sounded like a dog, or even a wolf,' said Boris.

We had nearly reached the park gate. As we approached the exit, five or six bristling shadows appeared in front of us. Girls with long, tangled hair. Boys with hats pulled low over their foreheads. They wore thick coats and had wolf masks over their faces, and carried spiky-looking sticks.

'Well, well. What have we here?' said one.

'New recruits!' said another. She sprang forward, ready to grab Johnny by the shoulders. But Amy was too quick for her. *Whoosh!* A beam of silvery light shot out from Amy's hand. The light formed a ball, encircling the wolf-girl completely. Amy raised her up, up, up into the air as the other wolves watched in horror – then hurled her into a clump of bushes at the edge of the park.

'Who's next?' said Amy. But the wolves had fled into the night.

'That's the Wolf Gang,' said Erwin. 'Another big gang here in Bristol.'

'We saw kids dressed as wolves,' I said slowly. 'When we left London.'

'They're all over the place now,' said Erwin.

'Better speed up,' muttered Teo.

'Yes,' said Erwin. 'There will be more.'

We jogged down the road. Most of the houses we passed were completely dark. At others, there was an occasional flicker of torchlight or lamplight in a window. Erwin had explained that the kids who hadn't joined a gang were too afraid to go outside or draw attention to themselves in any way. It was pretty quiet too. After a while, Teo led us into a warren of side streets. We'd be able to avoid the gangs more easily, she explained. The blood thumped in my ears as I ran. We had to be close enough to the bus station by now, I thought.

'Nearly there,' said Teo. 'It's... oh. Oh no.'

'What's wrong?' I said.

'Look,' she said, pointing.

The night sky was faintly alight with a reddish glow, and a thick cloud of smoke mingled with the snow clouds. I sniffed the cold air. Something was burning. Teo dropped her bag on the pavement and climbed halfway up a lamp-post to get a better look. Then, dejected, she jumped down. 'The bus station is on fire,' she said.

'Why?' said Jesse.

'Just the Looters having "fun", probably,' said Erwin. 'Looting, destroying. Why not burn buildings?'

'It's just annoying that those are the buildings we were trying to get to,' I said.

'We need another plan,' said Johnny, looking hopefully at a Range Rover. 'Amy, can you build a car? Or a bus?'

Amy laughed. 'I don't think my powers will go that far...'

Thwap!

'Yikes!' yelled Erwin, grabbing his ankle. I'd never heard anyone say 'Yikes' before, but Erwin really was rather strange.

Thwup! Thwap!

'Golf balls!' said Boris, grabbing Emma and pulling her into a doorway.

'Run, everyone!' I shouted.

'This way!' said Teo, heading off at a sprint down another side-street. I wanted to ask if she had a plan for where to go next but I was running too hard to be able to talk at the same time. Jesse and I helped Erwin along. He hadn't been badly wounded. After a time, the shots subsided, but I could hear feet thundering behind us and the shrill squeal of a referee's whistle.

'Is that the Golf Club?' I said.

'Unfortunately so,' said Erwin.

The snow was thickening, coming down fast and wet. We pelted down one street after another until the buildings thinned out and became bigger and more industrial and I realised that we'd come to the river. There were boathouses here and there, moored motorboats and canoes, peaceful and untouched in the water. Obviously, no gangs had bothered to come this way. Behind us, the shouting grew louder and louder. Team Storm raced down to the water's edge by a sign that said Bristol Boating.

'Um,' said Jesse. 'I don't think we should try to swim in this weather.'

Teo leapt down into a motorboat. 'Not swimming,' she said. 'Sailing.'

'Yes!' said Boris. He turned to Johnny. 'We've done this before in London, with a narrowboat.'

He closed his eyes for a second and I knew that he was thinking hard about the route.

'Can we get to Oxford by boat?' I asked.

'Ye-es,' said Boris again. He leafed through his atlas, marking pages with his fingers. 'Let me see... we'd need to get to Reading and then change rivers. But I'm sure we can figure out a way. And there won't be any traffic. Come on, team. Let's do this!'

One by one, we climbed down into the motorboat. It was a big one, quite expensive-looking, called the *Avon Queen*. It had a large canopy that you could sit underneath. Teo, Boris and Johnny huddled round the control panel. It looked complicated. 'Just... need... to get it started,' said Boris, hunting for a key, while Johnny and Teo pressed different buttons at random.

'There they are!' shouted a gravelly voice.

'Stop them!' came another out of the darkness. 'They can't leave. We need them to join the Golf Club and help defend the Earth from a second alien invasion!'

Erwin said, 'Oh, please. Anything but this.'

Thwap! Thwup!

'They're shooting at us!' screamed Emma, taking cover under a seat.

The golf balls hit the deck of the boat with hard, angry sounds. I peered through the snow. Now I could see the Golf Club – maybe ten or twelve kids, standing on the waterfront, all with golf clubs and peaked caps.

'Start the boat!' I said.

'I can't,' said Boris. 'There's no key.'

Freddie and Luke climbed onto the edge of the boat. 'Avast, you mangy marauders!' they yelled.

'Why are they talking like pirates?' asked Amy.

'I don't know,' I said. 'But look at what they're doing.'

Twanggg! Twonggg!

Freddie and Luke were serving the golf balls overarm with their tennis rackets, right back at the Golf Club, scattering them in all directions. Then Amy raised her hand and sent a ball of white light into their midst, sending the last few flying in mad, furious somersaults.

'Come back!' they yelled. 'We need you to join our club!'

'Sorry, guys,' shouted Erwin. 'The only club that I've ever cared to join is MENSA.'

Meanwhile, I flung myself at the controls and fished my silver Ankylosaurus out of my pocket. Would it work on a motorboat? There was only one way to find out...

With a click and a growl, the motorboat's engine came to life. Jesse untied the mooring rope. Johnny took the wheel. There really was nothing that kid couldn't drive. Freddie and Luke were still firing golf balls into the night sky as we pulled out of the harbour and set course down the River Avon, heading west.

'Erwin?' said Amy.

'Yes, my dear?' said Erwin.

'Was it true, what you just said about clubs?'

'I've been a member of MENSA since I was seven years old,' said Erwin. 'I definitely think you could join too, you know. If you wanted to. You're very intelligent.'

'I'll think about it,' said Amy. 'But I think you should reconsider your club-joining options. Because you are very definitely part of Team Storm.'

•

CHAPTER 15

Christ Church College

The *Avon Queen* chugged down the waterway in the icy dark. The sound of the engine was rhythmic and growly and seemed very loud; everything else was so silent. Swans turned their heads as we passed and I noticed Jesse smiling at them; I wondered if he was sending them messages. 'I miss Bill and Bruno,' he said, to no one in particular.

'Who?' said Johnny, at the wheel.

'The rhinos,' said Jesse. 'I wish I knew where they are now.'

Amy, Erwin, Freddie and Luke were fast asleep on the fold-down seats at the back of the motorboat. I was glad that they were getting some rest. I didn't plan to sleep myself; not until we'd made it to the MACE machine and brought the adults back safely. Teo was also awake, not saying anything, just staring at the shadowy shapes on the bank. From time to time she glanced at her mother's document, muttering to herself. 'Subatomic particles,' she said. 'Colour theory. Coloured light. I just don't know… What does it even mean?'

'You OK, Teo?' I said.

She shrugged. 'I'm thinking about what we're going to do when we get to the MACE machine. Will there be a switch, a button? Will it be obvious how to reverse the experiment?'

'Course it will,' said Boris. 'It'll be like, I dunno. Traffic lights. Red for stop and green for go.'

But Teo shook her head. 'Wells might have made it so that it can't be reversed at all. A toaster can't make toast into bread, can it?'

'Don't think like that,' I said. 'Your mum was sure it could be done.'

'She's an optimist. I'm a realist,' said Teo. 'Wells hated children. He wanted to create a perfect split between the two planes: two alternate realities. Why make it so that things could be changed back?'

'What does it say in the documents about reversing the process?' I said.

She sighed. 'Nothing. It doesn't say anything about it.'

We all fell silent, watching the snow land in drifts on the dark surface of the river.

Was Teo right? Would it be impossible to bring the adults back? I didn't know. Up until now, she'd been the one who was sure that we could do it. Now, she seemed to be losing heart. But still, we had to try. The next time I looked over at Teo, she was sound asleep, curled up around her rucksack. Boris had taken the wheel so that Johnny could do the same. 'You should get some sleep too, Oliver,' he said. 'You're the captain of Team Storm.'

'Exactly,' I said. 'I'll sleep when this is all over. Where are we now, Boris?'

'Bradford-on-Avon,' he said, after a pause.

'How long to go?'

'I dunno. Hours yet.' Boris looked at his watch. 'Midnight now. We ought to be there by morning, at this rate. I don't want to go faster than twenty knots, twenty-five tops. The water's too shallow to risk anything faster.'

'I see,' I said.

'So, Oliver. What do you think life will be like when the adults come back? D'you think it will be the same?'

I thought about this for a long time. Ice was beginning to form on the glassy surface of the river. We were going through some kind of lock, with thick trees on both banks. They were a bit like the forest outside

Oakwood Academy. Did I want to go back to Oakwood Academy? Did I want life to be the same as it had been before the yellow wave and the Great Disappearance? Yes, in some ways, and no, in other ways.

'I'm going to work harder in school,' said Boris. 'If the teachers come back, that is. I never thought I'd hear myself saying something like that.' He laughed, guiding the motorboat carefully through the narrow lock. 'I'm going to train to be a pilot, or a navigator or something. Something with maps.'

'I'm... I'm going to make a bit more effort with my dad,' I said, surprising myself just as much as I guessed Boris had surprised himself. 'I don't think things have been easy for Dad since Mum died. I always picture him as some kind of villain, but...'

'Didn't he expel you from Phoenix Feather High?'

'Well, yeah. But I think... I reckon we've just got into a bad pattern. Dad and me.'

'I get that,' said Boris. 'And, you know, I always thought your dad was pretty cool, back when we were at primary school together.'

'He was,' I said. 'He just changed after Mum died.'

Boris yawned widely. 'Hey, Oliver,' he said. 'If you're really not going to sleep, do you think you could take the wheel for an hour or so?'

'Sure,' I said. I'd never steered a motorboat before.

I watched closely as Boris showed me how to control direction and speed. And then, suddenly, they were all asleep – all nine other members of Team Storm – and it was just me and the boat and the water and the soft patter of snow overhead as we travelled on into the night.

In order to keep myself awake, I kept thinking, turning things over and over in my head. I thought about the MACE machine in that gloomy, dark room in Oxford, and the adults, trapped in their childless other dimension. I thought about Amy and her incredible new powers. I thought about all the people I now considered to be my friends: Boris, Jesse, Johnny, Emma, Teo, Freddie, Luke and Erwin. Only a few days ago, I hadn't really had that many friends. Not close ones. What did I think life would be like when the adults came back? I wasn't sure. But I was definitely going to make sure I kept my new friends.

At four thirty in the morning, it was still snowing as hard as ever when I looked up and saw what I thought were a couple of enormous birds in the sky overhead. Eagles, maybe? Hawks? I couldn't tell. They were high up, swooping in gigantic circles. Occasionally they let out long, creaky wails, like nothing I'd ever heard before. I almost wanted to slow down, to get a closer look at them, but after a while they disappeared from sight.

Not too long after that, we came to a kind of water junction where the River Kennet met the River Thames. Boris and Johnny woke up and came over to where I was standing at the helm. 'Nice one, Oliver,' said Johnny, slowing the boat down. 'I'll take it from here. We need to change course.'

I looked over to the seating area to see that Teo had woken up and was looking frantic. 'What's up?' I said.

'It's the time,' said Teo. 'It's already nearly six!'

'We'll be fine, surely,' said Johnny. 'We could just go faster.'

'I wouldn't,' said Boris. 'It's too risky. Look at the water. It's beginning to freeze.'

'OK,' I said. 'Let's get out here and find another way. A bus, maybe, or a van.'

'There's no guarantee that we'll find anything.' Teo was nearly in tears. The others were awake now, too, and gathering around us, their faces watchful and worried. Then Jesse looked up, gasped, and whistled loudly.

In a great snowy swirl, the rhinos came circling down, coming to land on the quayside of the marina, shaking snow from their hooves and cackling with delight at the sight of us.

'Bill! Bruno!' said Jesse, leaping off the boat and racing to pat their necks. 'Where did you go? Never mind. You're back and that's all that matters.'

Teo really was crying now, but with relief. We climbed off the motorboat and tied it to the quay. Then we piled on board the huge black bat-winged rhinos and took off into the snowy sky.

'Bye, *Avon Queen*,' yelled Johnny to the motorboat. 'You were a wonderful way to travel.'

We reached Oxford just as it was beginning to grow lighter. What a beautiful city it was; it looked like something out of an old fairy-tale. The streets and rooftops were blanketed in snow. There was not much green visible any longer. I looked for the tell-tale signs of armed gangs patrolling the streets. I couldn't see anyone anywhere, but I knew by now that first impressions of places could be deceiving. For a moment, my heart caught in my throat as I thought I saw a flash of blue. Could Eddie Sapphire have tracked us to Oxford? But no… it was only a balloon, tangled up in the bushes. The rhinos glided downward, taking us in a broad sweep over the colleges of Oxford. Then I saw some kids – not many, just a few – playing in the snow. They were oddly dressed in colourful hats. They didn't look like a gang. Not a bad one, anyway.

'That's Christ Church College there,' said Erwin,

after a few more minutes. 'Magnificent, isn't it?'

'It's incredible,' said Amy. 'The whole place is incredible.'

The rhinos started a steeper descent, so sharp that it felt like a roller-coaster ride. We came to land with a thud on a big snowy lawn closed on all sides by long pale buildings. We climbed down, blowing on our fingers to get them warm.

'Where should we go?' said Boris, looking at Erwin.

'Uh, I have no idea,' said Erwin. 'It's a big place.'

'We don't have a lot of time,' Teo said.

Amy was holding her hands in front of her, eyes closed. Then she opened them. 'I can feel it,' she said. 'It's here. It's very close.'

We all stared at her. What could she feel? Then Emma said, 'She's right. It's a kind of... vibration. In the air all around. Like a heat haze.'

Soon enough, I understood what Amy and Emma meant: there was something here in the college. Even the snow on the lawn was shimmering, as though it wasn't quite real, somehow. There was a feeling of electricity and excitement in the atmosphere, hard to describe but definitely, definitely there...

'Listen,' said Johnny. 'There's a hum. Hear it?'

Sure enough, there was a very, very slight humming sound. It reminded me of the time I had my teeth X-rayed. That kind of hum.

'It's coming from inside,' said Jesse, and off we went through the huge double doors into the college.

'Oh!' said Emma as we entered a large, dark hallway. 'What if it's a trap?'

I looked at her.

'Shouldn't we have brought some kind of weapon?' she said.

'We have our tennis rackets,' said Luke, brandishing his helpfully.

'Do rackets wear jackets?' asked Freddie.

'Look,' I said, 'if we start arming ourselves for battle... well, then we're no better than the gangs, are we? If we expect violence, then people will continue to behave violently. Team Storm is a peace-loving force for good in this world, and we will not be arming ourselves. There are other ways to fight.'

No one said anything to this. But I thought they all looked quite impressed. It was a pretty long speech for me. I'd never really made a speech before.

'Now let's go find the MACE machine,' I said.

Then I strode bravely off towards the humming sound. The others followed. Down corridor after corridor we walked, all of them dimly lit and hung with portraits of elderly, powerful-looking men and women. All the while, the humming grew steadily louder.

We went down a half-flight of polished steps, along a landing, and through a door marked RESEARCH WING: PRIVATE. Then up another flight of stairs, very narrow, and another, and along a winding, carpeted passage. Through a small round window, I could see the rhinos, charging about in the quad, playing in the snow. Now we were passing doors with numbers on them, and names. Professor Jillian Ziff. Professor Amos White. Professor...

Orwell Wells.

'This is it!' said Johnny, jumping up and down with excitement outside the ordinary-looking door. 'The sound is really loud now. It has to be here.'

And it was. A throbbing, thrumming, rhythmic hum. Like a machine. The MACE machine.

'Here we go,' I said, opening the door.

We filed in. It was totally dark inside. I felt for the light switch on the wall but, when I found it, it didn't seem to be working. 'Stay close together,' I whispered. It was pretty much impossible to see anything at all, apart from the machine itself in the middle of the room on a kind of platform. The machine was illuminated by a strange, luminous glow. The humming was really loud – not deafening, but very strong. Almost musical. I could actually see little waves of vibration coming off the shiny surface of the machine.

'Oh my God,' whispered Emma. 'Look at the timer on the screen.'

We crept closer. There, in red, was a digital timer, and it was counting down.

'We've only got twenty-nine minutes left,' whispered Jesse.

'But it's only about ten past eight!' said Boris. 'Why on earth...?'

'Because it wasn't a totally live broadcast,' said Teo. 'That's why. There was a time lag of twenty minutes or so. It seemed that the yellow wave hit just after 9am on Monday morning, but actually it happened earlier than that.'

Once again, I marvelled at the way Amy and Teo, who were so much younger than the rest of us, seemed to understand so much more than we did about scientific stuff.

'OK,' I said. 'We're going to do everything we can. But first we need some light in here.'

'I can do that,' said Amy. Holding up her hand, she summoned a ball of bright, swirly light and flung it up towards the ceiling, where it hovered like a lantern. Now we could see. The room was huge, much bigger than it had seemed on TV. Every wall was covered in dark wood and was lined with full suits of armour, perhaps forty or fifty of them. There was a long, old-fashioned mirror along one wall, in which we could see ourselves.

'I don't like those suits of armour,' said Emma. 'They're creepy.'

On the walls were glass display cases full of swords and old maps. I saw Boris glance at the maps with interest. There were three cameras: two on moving stands, and another hand-held one lying on its side, not far from the base of the machine. Adult clothing was scattered here and there. There was Professor Wells' white lab coat and clumpy boots; there were the black T-shirts and jeans and trainers of the camera crew. Teo knelt down by a pile consisting of a green tracksuit and yellow Converse and bright pink socks.

'Mum,' she whispered. 'Oh, we have to bring them back. Come on, Amy and Erwin. Let's look at the papers again.'

But Erwin was looking uncharacteristically miserable as he reached into his rucksack. 'I don't know how this happened,' he said, 'but – look.'

The documents from Dr Yang's study were soaked through by snow. They were totally unreadable.

'I'm sorry,' said Erwin. 'I guess the bag wasn't waterproof.'

'Don't worry,' said Amy kindly. 'We couldn't understand them anyway.' Then she looked thoughtful.

'Although there was something... something I think I almost understood...'

Meanwhile, the timer on the screen kept counting down. 24.57... 24.56...

We stood in an uneasy circle around the MACE machine. It glowed like radioactive lead. There were so many dials, switches, levers, buttons...

'Let's think,' said Teo. 'What did he do in order to activate the machine in the first place?'

'He flipped a couple of levers,' said Boris, pointing. 'This one, and this one. Then he pressed that big button there.'

'It was three levers,' said Jesse.

'No, it wasn't,' said Boris.

I frowned, trying to remember. 'Check on your iPad, Teo,' I suggested.

'Can't. Battery's flat,' she said. 'Besides, everything he did on TV could have been for show. There could have been other settings, other adjustments that the camera didn't pick up...'

'Oh, this is hopeless,' said Emma.

The timer counted down. Amy was kneeling, reading the tiny writing etched above the dials. 'Wavelength... Frequency...' she murmured. 'Plane division... Particle acceleration...'

Then she jumped up. 'This is all wrong,' she said.

'What's all wrong, Amy?' I said.

'This machine. It's too small. If Wells managed to split reality into two planes, he'd have needed something much, much bigger than this.'

'Of course,' said Erwin. 'Something like the Hadron Collider.'

'Sorry, what's that?' said Boris.

'It's a particle accelerator in Switzerland. It blasts subatomic particles at each other at high speed,' said Erwin. 'This machine in front of us is just a control unit. It can't possibly be the whole thing. Brilliant, Amy. I should have thought of that.'

'Do planes have brains?' asked Freddie.

'Do wires eat choirs?' asked Luke.

Amy stared at them. Then she said abruptly: 'Yes! Wires. Guys, quick. Follow the cables at the back of the machine. See where they lead.'

As quickly as we could, we fumbled with the wires at the back of the MACE machine, trying to figure out where they went. Some were attached to what looked like some kind of back-up power generator. Others went to a series of sockets at the wall. But there was one long cable with an unusual, rainbow-coloured flex that ran all along the floor, taped at intervals, and right under the enormous mirror on the opposite side of the room. I ran over and knelt down.

'Over here!' I yelled. 'There's something behind the mirror...' I pressed it in different places, feeling for a button or a switch. Nothing. Looking over my shoulder, I saw that we only had twenty-one minutes left.

Boris came up and gave the mirror a swift kick. 'That should do it,' he said.

And sure enough, the mirror slid backwards to reveal a space hollowed out of the wall, and a stairwell leading down into the ground. It reminded me of the entrance to some kind of bomb shelter. It was very narrow and very, very dark. I hesitated. 'Two teams,' I said. 'I'll head down there now with Boris, Teo and anyone else who wants to come. But we need people to stay here and stand guard.'

'OK, Oliver,' said Amy, still standing at the MACE machine control unit and scrutinising the dials. 'Hurry. Just go and have a look and tell us what we're dealing with.'

There was a slippery handrail and Boris, Teo, Erwin, Jesse, Freddie and I held it tightly as we descended into the basement of Christ Church College.

'Down, down, down,' said Freddie, who was, I thought, still quoting from *Alice in Wonderland*. 'Curiouser and curiouser,' he said.

He was right. The stairwell was leading us far beneath

the college now. All the while, the humming was getting louder and louder. It was almost deafening. We must have been going down for a good five minutes, perhaps more, when finally we came to a door marked NO ENTRY. I could see the rainbow-coloured cable running through a hole in the top of the door. I tried the handle. It was locked.

'Gentlemen,' said Boris, 'I've broken the rules for as long as I can remember. I feel that now would be a bad moment to break the habit of a lifetime.'

He kicked in the door, strode through it and...

'BORIS!' yelled Jesse. He lunged forward and caught hold of Boris, pulling him back just in time. On the other side of the door there was only a wooden platform about two metres square. And after that – nothing.

Nothing but empty space.

We were standing in a huge, hollow, black-as-night cavern. Big as a football stadium. Maybe bigger. I couldn't see the floor. It must have been miles beneath us. There was a ladder leading down from the platform, and that ladder led to what looked like a huge, circular machine. It was like a bicycle wheel. At the centre was a kind of mass of spinning circles of all different colours, and there were spokes of yellow light shooting out from the centre to the edges of the wheel. It made a churning, humming sound, almost musical.

'Woah,' breathed Freddie.

'That's the MACE machine,' said Erwin. 'We were right. I can't believe that Orwell Wells built something this size underneath an Oxford college.'

'I don't know whether it's terrifying or beautiful,' said Jesse.

'It's both,' said Teo. 'Science is like that.'

'I nearly fell into it,' said Boris. 'So that thing is what's creating the alternate dimension, where the adults are?'

'Yup,' said Erwin.

'Come on, guys,' I said. 'Let's get back upstairs and tell the others what we found.'

I was glad to head back up the stairs and away from the particle accelerator. It emitted a kind of weird, hypnotic power. I didn't want to be that close to it. How much time did we have left? Not long, I was sure. But was it long enough?

As we climbed out, breathless, into Professor Wells' room, I felt a sudden stab of anxiety. I'd left Amy on her own. What if something had happened?

'Amy!' I called out. 'You were right. It's a massive particle accelerator. Bigger than a football field. Like a huge yellow circle of light...'

'Oliver Storm,' said a rich, posh voice that I'd have known anywhere. 'At last, we meet again.'

Amy, Luke, Emma and Johnny were tied up, back to back, with strong-looking cords. Surrounding them were twelve or so members of the Blue Brigade, still in their sunglasses despite the gloom of the room. Looking around, I had a sudden realisation – they'd been there all the time, hiding behind the suits of armour.

And next to the MACE machine (or what we now knew was not the real MACE machine, just the control unit) was my old enemy, Eddie Sapphire.

'I'm so pleased to see you,' he said, smiling.

CHAPTER 16

•

The Reappearance

'Are you wondering how we found you this time?' said Eddie Sapphire, still with that same grin on his face, while the biggest and strongest of the Blue Brigade wrestled us to the round and tied us up incredibly tightly with rope. Now we were totally helpless. And the timer was still counting down.

There were only ten minutes remaining.

'Eddie, you have to let us go,' I said.

'Why should I do that?' said Eddie Sapphire. Lazily, he drew a finger along the shiny surface of the control unit. 'Pretty little thing, this machine. I was about to tell you how I found you. It was terribly easy.'

He strode towards me and reached for the collar of my shirt. Gently, he turned it inside-out and removed a tiny metallic disc, about the size of a ladybird.

'An ingenious little tracking device,' he said. 'I installed it when you so thoughtfully came up and punched me at the zoo. We caught up with you at Bristol. We captured your beasts – easier said than done, as a matter of fact, and rather annoyingly they escaped again – and then, when you got on your boat, we decided to follow you by road and see where you went. We knew, you see, that eventually you'd lead us here. To where it all started.'

I stared at him in fury. I couldn't believe that all this time, the Blue Brigade had been tracking our movements. It felt like something out of a spy movie. It was also really embarrassing. I was meant to be the leader of Team Storm, yet I hadn't noticed that Eddie Sapphire had planted a tracking device on me.

'Eddie, you idiot,' said Teo. 'If we don't figure out how to bring the adults back before that timer counts down to zero, we never will. The control unit is set to auto-destruct. Don't you get it?'

'I do get it,' said Eddie Sapphire. 'Which is why I can't let you mess with that machine. Why bring the adults back when the world is so much better without them? What have adults ever done except cause complications and unnecessary misery? I never met an adult who wasn't a complete fool.'

I realised that Eddie hated adults as much as Wells hated children.

'OK,' said Emma. 'So let's imagine they don't come back. Apart from the tragedy of never seeing any of the adults we love, ever again… Apart from the fact that it will be hard, maybe impossible, to run the world in a way that's decent and reasonable and fair and kind… Forget all that for a minute. You still have to realise, Eddie, that when you get to your eighteenth birthday, that's it. It's over. We saw it happen. A girl at Whipsnade just vanished before our eyes. In a couple of minutes, she was gone.'

A pause followed this. I could tell that Emma's words had made an impact. I could see Eddie Sapphire wavering, just for a second. Some members of the Blue Brigade started shifting about, as though they were also thinking about what Emma had said.

'Oh, well,' said Eddie, at last, 'I'm sure we'll be able to figure something out. Even if we don't, who cares? I don't want to be a grown-up anyway.'

'Don't you want to see your parents again?' said Jesse.

'I despise my parents,' said Eddie Sapphire.

'He's crazy,' whispered Johnny. 'He's utterly crazy.'

But the Blue Brigade were beginning to look troubled. 'Mr Sapphire, sir,' said one of them. 'I… I don't know if I want to go along with this, after all. If the machine self-destructs…'

'Silence, Henry!' shouted Eddie. 'Don't be a rotten coward.'

Bridget stepped forward. 'He's right,' she said.

She took off her sunglasses. I realised she wasn't actually that grumpy-looking. Just anxious. 'At first, I thought it was great,' she said. 'All my life, I never felt I had control of anything. I never belonged anywhere before. Then we were running Luton Airport. It was awesome. Finally, I was part of a team. And then it became this mad, exciting game, chasing this lot around the country, trying to stop them from bringing back the adults. But, now that we're here... now that it's real... I miss my parents. I miss my gran.'

One by one, the Blue Brigade were shrugging off their long blue reflective jackets.

'I order you to stand down!' yelled Eddie Sapphire, jumping up and down with rage.

But they ignored him. Bridget and Henry cut our ropes and released us. Eddie stopped jumping up and down and stood, fists clenched, flabbergasted, as though he couldn't believe what was happening.

Boris walked over and stood close to him. 'If you try to stop us from doing what we have to do, I'll punch you in the face,' he said, in a friendly, conversational way. 'And I promise you, I hit harder than Oliver does.'

Eddie Sapphire screamed some further obscenities (which I won't record here) at the Blue Brigade, then turned around and fled from the room, shrieking and sobbing. Minutes later, we watched through the window as he ran in a deranged zigzag through the snow in the courtyard below.

'They'll all suffer!' we heard him yelling to the rhinos, who gazed at him in bafflement.

And then Eddie Sapphire was gone.

'Oh, thank God,' said Emma.

We had four minutes left.

Amy was moving her hands over the control unit, examining the dials again. 'Think, Amy, think,' she murmured.

'What readings do you see on the dials?' said Erwin.

'Plane division: FULL,' read Amy. 'The wavelength dial is at 580nm. The frequency is 512Thz,' she went on.

'What does that mean?' I said.

'Nm stands for nanometre,' said Teo. 'Thz stands for terahertz.'

'Means nothing to me,' said Boris.

'They do mean something,' said Amy. 'I'm thinking... Your mum said Professor Wells was working with colour theory, right?'

'Right,' said Teo. 'He was interested in coloured light.'

'Three minutes,' said Johnny.

Amy's eyes were shining in a way that told me that she'd thought of something. 'And... and... Oliver, you said the particle accelerator was really colourful and bright, right?'

'Right,' I said. 'Lots of colours sort of zooming about everywhere, but mostly...'

'YELLOW,' said Amy. 'These readings are for yellow light. And what happened when the adults disappeared?'

'A yellow wave!' we chorused.

'Wow,' I whispered.

'Yellower and yellower,' said Luke helpfully, pinging a string on his tennis racket.

Amy grabbed a pencil and started scribbling on a piece of paper. 'In order to successfully split the known universe into two parallel planes, Wells used the frequencies of yellow light in conjunction with the particle accelerator to somehow – I don't know how – separate the children and the adults. It sounds crazy, but... but that's what he did. So what's the opposite of yellow?'

'Indigo,' said Jesse.

'On a conventional colour wheel, yes,' said Erwin. 'But light is different. The opposite of yellow light is blue light.'

'Are you sure about that?' I asked.

'I'm a certified genius,' said Erwin shortly. 'Of course I'm sure.'

'So... we need to create a blue wave,' said Amy. 'Teo, help me.'

The rest of Team Storm stood round, amazed,

as Amy and Teo adjusted the dials. Teo was shaking. 'What if we break the machine?'

Amy shrugged. 'This is the only chance we're ever going to get. It has to be now.'

'Ninety seconds,' said Johnny.

'Let's turn wavelength down a bit more,' said Teo. 'And frequency up a bit more. No, sorry. Wrong way round. Oh God, I'm so nervous.'

'Now we prepare to reset the machine,' said Amy. She turned three more dials up to full capacity, and the plane division dial down to zero.

'Thirty seconds,' said Johnny.

'Ready, Oliver?' said Amy, indicating a big green RESET button on the side of the control unit.

'Why me?' I said.

'Because you're the leader,' said Emma.

'Huh,' I said. 'You just want it to be my fault if it all goes wrong.'

'Just do it!' said Teo.

'OK.' I breathed out heavily through my nose. 'OK. Here goes.'

'Good luck,' said the boys and girls who had once been known as the Blue Brigade.

'Good luck,' said Team Storm.

'Good luck,' I said to myself. I stretched my finger out to the RESET button.

I thought about Dad and Britney, all the teachers and random other adults I'd ever known, and the parents and guardians of Team Storm. I thought about the Wolf Gang and the Golf Club and the Zoo Tribe and the Blue Brigade and all the children, all over the country, who were lost and lonely and helpless and desperately wishing they could see their parents again. I thought about being a leader and how it meant that sometimes you have to do things that are totally and completely terrifying.

Like pressing a big green button.

'Five seconds,' said Johnny. The humming grew louder and louder, as though a hive of bees was about to burst forth into an angry swarm...

The tip of my finger touched the surface of the button.

I pressed down. Hard.

And the world was swallowed up in a gigantic wave of brightest blue.

•

I don't know how long we all stayed huddled together by the MACE machine control unit while the blue smoke swirled around us.

'Did it work?' said Amy, in a small voice.

'Well, we're all still here,' said Jesse. 'But...'

'What the blazes just happened?' said another voice that I didn't recognise.

'Isn't it obvious?' said a cross-sounding voice that I thought I did recognise, though I wasn't sure whose it was.

'Oh!' said someone else. 'We're naked again.'

The vivid blue smoke began to fade and finally we could see.

'Three... two... one... zero,' said Johnny, who still had his eye on the timer. There was a low *phuttt* and a slow *whirr*, and the MACE machine control unit switched off. Just like that.

'We were only just in time,' I heard Emma say.

'MUM!' screamed Teo. I looked over to see Teo fling her arms around the neck of a very pretty, dark-haired woman who was completely naked. So that was Caitlin Yang. There were two rather disgruntled-looking men with grey hair, naked as well, and a few another men and women. Also naked. And – just as strange as he'd appeared on TV, and just as angry – Professor Orwell Wells. Naked.

'I knew you'd figure out a way, my darling,' said Dr Yang.

'It wasn't just me,' said Teo. 'It was all of us. Team Storm.'

Teo's mum looked at us all. 'Erwin! You're here too. Thank goodness.'

'Hi, Dr Yang,' said Erwin.

'I thought you didn't like teams, Teo,' said Dr Yang.

'I do now,' said Teo, winking at Amy, who winked back.

'Will someone please explain what on earth is happening?' bellowed one of the disgruntled-looking elderly men. 'This is my college, for goodness' sake.'

'Blimey, it's freezing in here,' said one of the women.

Then, with the coordination that they'd learnt after three days of being the Blue Brigade, Henry and Bridget and the other kids who had once answered to Eddie Sapphire picked up their long blue coats and handed them to the adults. They were received very gratefully. It isn't much fun being naked in a freezing cold room at any time, but it must have been doubly difficult for them at that moment. We'd just brought them back from an alternate reality, after all.

I thought, as leader of Team Storm, that maybe I should explain.

'Hello,' I said. 'I'm Oliver Storm. This is my team. And this lot is another gang... I mean, team, who've recently joined us. We've just brought you back from an alternate dimension – a kind of parallel plane – which

196

Professor Wells created with a particle amalgamator...'

'A particle accelerator,' said Teo. 'Right here. Below this university.'

There were general cries of astonishment.

'I told you that,' said Professor Wells mildly, to the now not-naked people. Then he looked at us. 'Personally, I am astonished that you children worked out how to reverse the experiment. I myself wasn't sure it could be done. Certainly, it couldn't from my side. When I split reality into two identical planes, some things happened that I expected, such as the fact that the people who were removed from this side ended up totally naked afterwards. Clothes can't cross the border between planes.'

At this, the adults looked even more disgruntled and resentful.

'But one thing I didn't expect,' said Wells, 'was that the particle accelerator itself – the MACE machine, that these children discovered below the basement – would remain on their side. Perhaps a machine of such complexity, which was actually generating the division of the planes, couldn't possibly be duplicated.'

He walked up to us slowly, looking at each of our faces. 'How did you do it?' he said.

'We knew you were working with coloured light,' said Amy. 'I should have realised before that the yellow wave was yellow for a reason. Somehow, you connected the frequency of yellow light to your particle accelerator, with the result that you were able to divide adults and children into two separate worlds.'

My eight-year-old sister is talking, easily and without embarrassment, to a bunch of grown-ups in long blue jackets, I thought in amazement.

'So, to reverse the experiment, we turned the yellow wave blue,' said Amy. 'Blue light being the opposite of yellow light.'

'Well, well,' said a dark-haired man with a neat moustache. 'We have you to thank, then. All of you. A world without children would have been a tragedy that none of us could have ever comprehended.'

Jesse was staring at him. 'You're the Prime Minister, Mortimer Bruce,' he said. 'Sorry. I didn't recognise you with no clothes on.'

The Prime Minister looked like he was trying not to burst into laughter at that. 'Three days we've been waiting in this room, in the hope that someone from the other side would be able to change things back to the way they were. But when Wells here told us he'd built a self-destruct function into the controls, we weren't sure that anyone would manage anything within that time. What you children have done... it's simply magnificent.'

'Have you been all right, all on your own?' said a woman who I decided was the Prime Minister's wife.

We looked at each other. 'Yes and no,' said Emma.

'We were going to run out of food sooner or later,' said Jesse.

'Some of us developed weird powers,' I said, thinking of Amy.

'And some of us joined strange gangs,' said Bridget.

'We missed the grown-ups,' said Teo, still with her arms around her mother.

'I must ring Melissa and Jack,' said the Prime Minister's wife, rushing out. I assumed she was talking about her children.

'We'll do a national broadcast on all channels and stations,' said a woman with bright green eyes. 'Let as many people as possible know what's going on. I'm the Head of the BBC,' she added, for our benefit.

'Anything will be better than your last broadcast, Jane,' said the Prime Minister.

The Head of the BBC looked sulkily at Professor Wells. 'We were told it was a live experiment to reduce harmful carbon dioxide emissions. Wells was very convincing.'

Orwell Wells shrugged. 'I couldn't have told you the truth, could I? I had to tell you something that you'd believe.'

Now that he was actually standing there, he didn't look like a big, powerful, crazy scientist any longer. He looked slightly pathetic. I almost felt sorry for him.

'Orwell,' said Teo's mum. 'You're a brilliant scientist. You've created a machine the likes of which no one has ever seen before. Let's find ways to use your MACE machine for some other purpose. Something good. What do you say?'

'Well, perhaps,' said Professor Wells. 'You know what, I always thought I couldn't stand children. But honestly, for the past few days, in a world run solely by adults... I've been bored. I missed being annoyed by sulky teenagers with unwashed hair... Children who stick their tongue out at me through the rear window of their parents' car... My rather sweet niece and nephew.'

He smiled. 'It was a fascinating experiment,' he said. 'But I'm glad it has come to an end. And – who knows, perhaps I shall be awarded the Nobel Prize for Physics!'

Team Storm looked at each other.

'Totally crazy,' muttered Johnny.

'I'm afraid, Professor Wells, that – Nobel Prize or not – you're still under arrest,' said a woman with short dark hair. I realised that she was a police officer.

'Separating the world's children from their parents is a major criminal offence,' added a tall man who must also have been a police officer.

Taking a mildly protesting Wells by the arms, they ushered him out of the room. The Head of the BBC, the Dean of the College and the Prime Minister were deep in conversation. Teo's mum gathered the Blue Brigade and Team Storm around her.

'My darlings,' she said. 'It's time we all went home.'

·

CHAPTER 17

One Month Later

Amy and I were having breakfast with Dad and Britney before school. Same house, same kitchen, same view through the window – just a little less wintry. Spring was around the corner. The porridge was the same, although I was eating it with a dollop of maple syrup, which improved it loads.

But so much was different.

'More juice, Oliver?' said Dad, with a smile. Ever since I, along with the rest of Team Storm, had been made a Member of the British Empire for Services to the Entire World, Dad had finally decided to forget about the toilet-flooding incident at Phoenix Feather High. He had even gone so far as to acknowledge that – just maybe – he had been wrong to expel me. 'First impressions can be deceiving,' he'd said, several times. 'I should have known better than to judge my own son so harshly.'

As Dad topped up my orange juice, I smiled back. I remembered the conversation I'd had with Boris on board the *Avon Queen*. Two people have to make an effort in order for a relationship to change. Not just one.

I watched Amy over the cereal boxes. She was staring at a bunch of flowers on the kitchen table.

'Hey, Amy,' I said. 'What are you thinking?'

She sighed. 'I was trying to move the flowers,' she said.

'I thought you were,' I said sympathetically.

'I do miss my powers,' my little sister said.

'But, Amy,' I said, 'you didn't use your powers to bring the adults back. You used your brain. Your amazing brain. No one can ever take that away from you.'

She looked more cheerful. 'Do you think they'll ever let Wells out of prison?'

'I dunno,' I said. 'But Dr Yang is doing some awesome research with the MACE machine, now that they've moved it to the countryside. We can go and visit again at the weekend, if you like.'

'Yes, definitely,' she said. 'I want to see Teo and Erwin.'

Teo and Erwin spent every weekend working at the MACE project's new headquarters. There was a new global initiative to get kids more involved in adult jobs and seeing how everything operates.

'I want to see Freddie and Luke,' I said. 'I sort of miss them. Even though they are a bit weird.'

'They're weird in a good way,' said Amy seriously. 'They started an official *Alice in Wonderland* Appreciation Society. I hear it's very successful.'

'Time for school,' said Britney, handing us our lunchboxes.

•

Amy still went to St Hearts Junior School. But now she had loads of friends. It wasn't just that she was a bit famous, like we all were, in the weeks that followed the return of the adults. It was the fact that Amy had changed from a timid little girl who was scared of most people to someone who knew exactly who she was and what she wanted to do. It made me so happy, seeing her go skipping off to school every day, organising play-dates and chatting to her friends on Skype in the evenings.

'Bye, Oliver,' she said, giving me an enormous hug.

She drove off with Dad, as usual, in the direction of St Hearts, while Britney and I got into Britney's car. I had my rucksack, my iPhone, a few snacks, a water bottle, my lunch, and, of course, my Ankylosaurus.

It had really been a very lucky mascot indeed.

The gates of Oakwood Academy stood wide open. There was no longer a manned security checkpoint at entry, just a couple of cheerful-looking staff members in bright blazers, greeting people as they drove in.

'Morning, Oliver. Morning, Mrs Storm,' they said.

As we went up the steps to the doors, underneath a huge banner saying WELCOME TO OAKWOOD that was covered in tiny sparkly flowers, my stepmother said, 'You know, Oliver, I hated this place so much when I started teaching here. I didn't think I could possibly continue. But now, after Wells' experiment, it's really become... Well, what do you think?'

'It's not bad,' I said. 'Really not bad at all.'

It was true that Oakwood Academy was now a rather different place. When Principal Brown returned, along with the rest of the adults, he returned with a dramatically different view of the world. He no longer wanted to impose so many rules on the kids at his school. He no longer wanted it to be a strict, joyless institution.

He had explained all this to us once the school was fully functioning again and they'd tidied up all the mess.

'From now on,' he told us at assembly, 'you will not have to pay to use the toilet. You will, of course, be refunded for anything you have spent so far.

And laughing in the corridors is one hundred per cent permitted. Indeed, it is ENCOURAGED!'

We all cheered loudly at this.

'Oh, and one more thing,' said Principal Brown, who had also un-fired all the teachers that he'd got rid of in recent months. 'Oakwood Academy will, from this point forward, be accepting girls.'

At this, we cheered even more loudly.

I was remembering this and still feeling pleased as Britney and I headed up to the 11B form room. Boris was already there, doing some geography homework. He looked up when he saw me, and smiled. Jesse was there too. Not surprisingly, Jesse had realised that he wanted to become a vet – ideally, one who works with animals abroad. He had stayed in touch with many members of the Zoo Tribe. They'd all returned home now, even Paloma, who, it turned out, hadn't vanished forever after all. On her eighteenth birthday, she (and several thousand others) simply got dragged over into the adults' dimension. Paloma described it in an email to Jesse as 'weird and a bit uncomfortable, but not painful'. And every other weekend, Jesse went to Whipsnade to see Bill and Bruno. They no longer had wings, but they were, he assured me, the best rhinos in the world.

'How's Johnny, Boris?' I said.

'He's great. Hasn't been in detention once,' said Boris.

'He's helping to run a driving school for under-17s on a large country estate just outside London, teaching kids to drive. He loves it, as you can imagine.'

'Cool,' I said, sitting down next to a girl with bright-orange hair tied back in a ponytail. 'And how are you doing?'

'Enjoying my new school,' Emma said. 'It's not nearly as bad here as you made out, Oliver.'

'Well, it's improved loads since the Great Disappearance,' I said. I was really glad that Emma had joined Oakwood Academy and was no longer home-schooled at the Holiday Inn. Seeing Emma was always one of the highlights of my day. It was really cool that Team Storm still got to hang out together. But I wasn't the leader any more. Now, we were all just friends. Maybe one day I'd be a leader again. We'd just have to see. Sometimes, I wondered what had happened to Eddie Sapphire. Would our paths ever cross in the future?

Again, we would just have to see.

'Right, kids,' said Britney. 'You've got science first lesson.'

'Yes, Mrs Storm,' we said, picking up our stuff.

'Have a good time. Who knows – maybe something life-changing and incredible will happen? Some kind of earth-shattering experiment, perhaps?'

My stepmother looked at me, and winked.

The whole class burst out laughing.